My name is Cherry Delight. I am just what the name implies, a delightful redhead. I work for N.Y.M.P.H.O. (THE NEW YORK MAFIA PRO-SECUTION AND HARASSMENT ORGANIZA-TION. I double as call girl and killer, spy and seduc-tress. I have been trained to crack a safe or a skull, pick a pocket like a pro, or to fight in a variety of ways, including judo, karate, and even Burmese box-ing. I can speak six languages. Using a revolver or automatic, I can hit a bulleye nine times out of ten. Against me the Mafia doesn't have a chance.

CHERRY DELIGHT #1

THE ITALIAN CONNECTION

GLEN CHASE

(Gardner F. Fox)

FICTION HOUSE PRESS

First Published in 1972 by Nordon Publications Inc.

First Fiction House Edition January 2021

isbn 9781-64720-208-8

Fiction House Press
www.FictionHousePress.com

Chapter One

I lay naked in my coffin.

However, I was very much alive. My big brown nipples were standing up so stiffly, they actually ached. And my genital folds were positively twitching in sexual excitement, to say nothing of my slightly oversized clitoris which was poking up between those scarlet lips.

Now believe it or not, I was hard at work.

Fact! But since I work for N.Y.M.P.H.O.—the New York Mafia Prosecution and Harassment Organization—some of my work takes me into the damndest places. Like this expensive silver and mahogany coffin, for instance.

The handsome young man with the feather in his hand with which he had been tickling my rather large mammaries and my even more intimate private parts, drew a sobbing breath. Mark Condon is my contact man with N.Y.M.P.H.O., which means he brings me the orders which the bossman of the organization, called The Controller, wants me to carry out.

Right now he was drawing the ticklish fronds of that ostrich feather up and down my girlish body, pleasing me no end and getting me in the mood for polite rape. You see, I had a date with a Cosa Nostra member and everybody, including the Cosa Nostra boy himself, wanted me in the right mood. His eyes were bugging out as he saw how hard my breasts were, how my slight mound of belly quivered when he ran the feather over it, and the way my pubic hair bristled as those fronds became extremely intimate with certain personal possessions of mine.

"You s-sure you k-know what to do?" he panted.

"Relax, already," I told him, smiling sweetly. "You've done your part of the job, you've gotten me in the mood for fun and games."

He had gotten himself in the mood, too, I saw as I sat up in the coffin and peered over the edge of what was standing at attention in his glen plaid slacks. Ordinarily, I'd have been more than willing to fry his bacon for him, but we had no time for fooling around. I had to be shipped across town to the Giuseppe Turessi Funeral Home within the hour. I felt sorry for Mark, it really was hard on him, playing with my nudity like this, but it was part of his job.

My name is Cherry Delight. Okay, okay. I was baptised Cherise Dellissio, but friends and lovers have since tabbed me with the more euphonious Cherry Delight. And I love it, because it's true. I am just what the name implies, a delightful red-headed pussy. I am also a member of the Femmes Fatales, that special branch of N.Y.M.P.H.O. which consists of a few very, especially selected sexy girl operatives whose job is that of call girl and killer, spy girl and seductress.

I have also been trained to crack a safe, to pick a pocket as neatly as any professional dip, to fight in an assorted varieties of ways, including judo, karate, and even Burmese boxing. I can talk half a dozen languages, I'm able to hit the bullseye with a revolver or automatic nine times out of ten, and I'm reasonably expert in any field you can name that might help me against the crime lords. As a result, I'm unleashed like a hunting hound when there is a need for my services.

Like now.

Our enemy is the Mafia, that underworld branch of a Sicilian society that has spread out across our world. It makes its money from vice and prostitution, from gambling and the numbers rackets, from protection payments, from takeovers of legitimate businesses, usually by threats and intimidation, from drugs, from usury, and from whatever else that turns a buck. I'd stake my sweet life that the Mafia even runs a number of governments.

It is very hard, if not downright impossible, to fight an organization like that by recognized legal means. Police and judges have been known to take bribes, and witnesses are often murdered or threatened, so the legal remedies of court trial by jury are worthless. Even if you bring in a few members and get a conviction, others spring up to take their places.

The Mafia operates outside the law, so the only way to fight them is to play the game by their own rules. Which is why the New York Mafia Prosecution and Harassment Organization was formed. It works with Federal and local agencies in the United States and outside its boundaries, it has contacts with Scotland Yard and the Surete, with Interpol and the police forces of quite a few nations. A N.Y.M.P.H.O. agent is given carte blanche to get the job done, no matter who gets hurt in the process, and with no questions asked about the legality of method.

Which brings me into a coffin.

The Turessi Funeral Home was suspect. My organization had it tabbed as a meeting place for gangsters, an unofficial headquarters where information and mob secrets were gathered, sorted out and then relayed on to the big bosses. Now the real control of the Mob is not here in Uncle Sam land, it's in Europe. Where? Who knows? Part of my job was to find that real boss of bosses and to eliminate him.

The Controller figured that if I could scratch the Mafia chief, it might thrown the rest of their outfit into a power struggle for the top spot. This would give the police departments of the world a little breathing room.

There was more to it than a search out and destroy mission, however. We people from N.Y.M.P.H.O. use wiretapping and underworld informers to keep us abreast of what's going on. And we'd heard via the goon grapevine that something big was in the wind. The Mafia boss of bosses had his grubby paws on some kind of gadget that would make our own job harder than ever.

What it was, nobody on our side knew.

This was where Cherry Delight, Mafia Hunter, got to run with the hounds. It was my job to learn what that gadget was and to lay hands on it while at the same time—if at all possible—I must prevent the crime lords from using it for their own ends.

First of all, I had to get into that mortuary. Alive, naturally. This part of it was easy, because Giuseppe Turessi who runs the joint, had asked for a Femme Fatale. So I was being shipped naked and with a case of the hots to Joe baby, whose taste in females was something more than notorious.

So why a coffin? Well, Joe Turessi was a boss, which was pretty high up in the 'confederation family' of Mafia crime lords. He also had a bit of a sexual fetish of which he was ashamed. Besides, he didn't trust his Mob brothers, he was afraid they'd rat on him if word got about what he did in a certain upstairs room of the funeral home. The boss of bosses might think him ripe for sexual blackmail and have him removed, which means killed, in this instance. So he made certain arrangements with Femme Fatales, and here I was. Joe Baby liked his job and wanted to keep it.

Since our N.Y.M.P.H.O. boys had been on his trail for some time, they didn't want him replaced, either; it would have meant a lot of work getting to know and understand his replacement. So my N.Y.M.P.H.O. bosses decided that they'd play along with him and send him his call girl in a coffin.

The coffin was my cover, in more senses than one. What's more natural to ship to a mortuary than a coffin, outside maybe a dead body? My pink nudity would be delivered to Joe Turessi, he would lift the coffin lid and out I'd pop like an entertainer from a cake at a convention. A cute redhaired pussy present for a Mafia boss.

Of course, the coffin was fitted out with a can of oxygen and an inhalator, and here and there cleverly hidden holes had been made so that fresh air would come in. The silken lining of the coffin was zippered, I could push it down and out of the way so I wouldn't suffocate.

The feather was drifting idly back and forth between my thighs, up against my labial folds. My hips lurched, my breath came faster, faster. I couldn't help the low moan rising from between my parted lips.

"Damn you, Mark," I breathed. "Stop torturing me."

"The Controller said to tease you good," he panted.

His eyes were fastened on my big breasts which were like water-filled balloons, right about now. My brown nipples were up so high they hurt. That damned ostrich feather was like hands and lips traveling all over my nudity. If the Controller wanted to make sure I gave Joe baby so good a time that he'd take me with him to Europe, he sure knew how to get Mark Condon to go about it.

Mark was suffering too. His blue eyes were like glass and the sweatbeads on his brow were even more pronounced. The hand that held the feather was shaking. And down there in his pants, his male member was standing at full attention.

Any other time I would have hopped out of that damn coffin and onto that rigid meat-bar, but duty is duty. I had a case of the hots that musn't be wasted on Mark Condon. It had to be used to make myself indispensable to Giuseppe Turessi. He just had to take me to Europe with him.

"Please. Close the lid. Let's get going," I whispered.

Mark licked his lips, nodded.

He tossed aside the feather, lifted his hands to the lid and slowly brought it down, closing off the world. I lay in darkness, shivering faintly. Sure, sure. I was hotted up, but I was also being sealed inside a coffin, not quite sure whether I would ever come out of it.

I knew how important my job was, I was gung-ho on seeing it through. Just the same, I was cut off from the world around me and morbid fancies began trotting through my head. Suppose somebody made a mistake and thought mine was a dead body? Maybe this Joe Turessi was a smarter guy than N.Y.M.P.H.O. believed him to be, he might guess I wasn't just a call girl but a secret agent working for an anti-crime organization. In which case, he might nail shut the coffin lid and send me to some cemetery.

I felt the coffin being rolled along the floor, lifted and carried. It was slid into a delivery truck. I heard the truck motor revved to life, felt the truck begin to move. I quieted a little, telling myself the ride would not take more than thirty minutes, a mere half hour.

I closed my eyes. It would be nice to drift off to sleep, to be awakened by an amorous man. But who the hell could sleep? I didn't want to be buried alive. I love life, the things the world can offer a healthy, vital girl-girl. I twisted restlessly inside the coffin, it seemed I could not breathe.

My hand reached for the inhalator, fumbled it to

my face. I turned the valve and breathed deeply. The cool oxygen felt good to my lungs, it soothed me. I quieted and lay motionless. The trip could not take much longer, I told myself. After all, a half hour isn't very long. And yet it was an eternity.

All things come to an end, though. Even such a ride as this, with me sweating inside that coffin and telling myself I was an idiot to have become a member of the N.Y.M.P.H.O. team and most especially, its Femmes Fatales branch. I could have had a nice, safe job as somebody's personal secretary, somewhere or other.

The truck jerked to a stop.

I held my breath. Would I feel the thud of a hammer and nails on the coffin lid, nailing me in there forever? No! The coffin began its slide down the truck floor, it was lifted out, carried.

The coffin was set down.

This was the moment of reckoning. It was now that the nails would come thudding into the lid, if Joe Turessi suspected who I was and why I was here in his mortuary. There was a long silence. Come on, come on! my mind screamed. Let's get this show on the road.

The lid rose up. I found myself staring into the flushed face of a middle-aged man, his black hair dusty with grey, as was his tiny moustache, while his sideburns were flecked with white. But his black eyes were alive, roving across my big breasts as if kissing them. They slid down my pink-skinned belly to my fluffy red Venus boskage. His tongue came out and went around his full lips.

"You darling," I breathed, reading his thoughts.

I did a little shimmy, making my breasts slide back and forth. The lust fever which Mark Condon had put in my erogenous zones with that ostrich feather was about to be satisfied. My bare arms came up, I slid inside the coffin until I was sitting up.

Joe baby reached for my hands, eyes sparkling. He had a hump hunger inside him that told me he liked what he saw as I gave my hands to his and lifted upward in the coffin until I was standing stark naked in front of him.

I bent forward, my breasts dangling, bloated with rut need, swollen into huge, blue-veined love jugs. The nipples were long, thick. I bent a little more, brushed his flushed face with my titties. Joe Turessi groaned.

"I want this to last a long time," I whispered, almost smothering him in the masses of my breasts.

"You betcha, kid. Me, too."

He was not the slick, polished Mafia member I had expected. There was a part of the ghetto still inside Joe Turessi, and it showed. His tiny moustache tickled my nipples as he moved his face back and forth, kissing my breastflesh. My eyes went down to his striped trousers. He had what the French call *pine d'officher*. In other words, his erection was making like a tentpole in his pants.

I lifted one leg upward, as if looking for a place to step. His eyes widened as they slid up my inner thighs right to the scarlet folds of my pussy, half hidden in crisp red genital hairs. I posed like that while his tongue came out again to run around his mouth.

"You're teasing me, doing that," I whispered.

He caught on fast, saying, "I like do that to you, kid. I'd like to get in there between those swell gams of yours and show you how I can work my tongue."

"But not yet?"

He laughed softly. "Not yet, nah. I'm gonna take my time. Ya see, I like to watch. I wanna see you walkin' around bareass and then wearin' clothes. It's kind of a thing with me."

"Oooooh, you make it sound so exciting!"

"It'll be exciting, kid. You wait'n see."

He cupped his hands, offering them as a stirrup for my foot. I put my bare toes in his palms, leaned forward and began to slide downward. Of course, since he was so close, my bare legs brushed his face all the way up to my pubic hairs. His lips nestled amid those hairs for a brief moment, I felt his lips kissing, then his tongue giving my wet folds a little lick.

"That feels terrif," I panted, rubbing back and forth against his face.

It did, too. After what Mark Condon had done to

me, I was ready to indulge this man in any kind of sex he wanted. I think he sensed this because he drew back his head and stared up at me with slightly bulging eyes.

"I ain't begun yet, kid. Wait'll I really get goin' on ya. I'm gonna eat that hair pie of yours like nothin' you ever felt. You're the kinda doll I go for!"

Score points for my side. Well, this was why I was here, to rack up so many Brownie points that Joe Turessi wouldn't be able to do without me and the agamuniacal attentions I would give him. It was the name of my game. Then he would invite me to accompany him to Europe so I could lay hands on whatever it was he was going to Europe to get from his fellow Mafia mobsters.

As I say, this was the battle plan.

I set myself to bring it to fruition. I slid down on my middle-aged lover boy until my perfumed bellyflesh was against his lips and he was covering that flesh with kisses and tongue-licks. He was panting hard, I could see the sweatbeads on his high forehead.

Down I went until his lips closed over one of my nipples and drew it deep into his warm, wet mouth. He suckled slowly, lovingly. I tabbed Joe Turessi for a mouth man, he liked to get his lips and tongue on any part of the female anatomy that attracted him.

The other breast now. His teeth bit gently into the base of my thickly swollen nipple as he tugged the rest of it deep into his mouth. He was quivering, standing here with his arms wrapped about my slim middle, feasting on my titties. When he loosened the grip of his arms I slid down a little more, threw my arms around his neck and placed my open lips on his.

We French-kissed like that a long time.

His eyes were glassy when we parted. "I ain't never met nobody like you before, kid. I go for you. I really do. You're something else, real special."

"I want to be—for you," I whispered, kissing him hungrily. "But you mentioned clothes, honey. What kind of clothes?"

Sex has many aspects. Turessi might be a sadist, in which case those clothes would hurt, in some way. There would be something tight for my breasts, something rough to chafe my tender pussylips. But I didn't exactly think so. Joe Turessi was getting his jollies just by kissing and licking me. This told me he wasn't a sadist.

So I opted for the fact that he was a voyeur.

He liked to see women in sexy garments. Nothing wrong with that. What male doesn't? I knew how to handle his kind, all right. And if he had some especially nice undergarments, maybe he'd give them to me to take to Europe with him. If he asked me to go with him, that is. It was my job to make sure he did.

My bare feet rested on the cold floor tiles. I pretended to shiver, causing my breasts to do their sliding jig back and forth, then up and down. Joe baby ate them with his eyes.

"Brrr! It's cold here," I half laughed.

He slapped his forehead with a palm. "I'm sorry. I been so selfish, looking at you all naked, it's a damn shame to cover you up. You're great without clothes."

"But chilly."

His hand caught mine, brought me at the run with him across the floor of the mortuary storage room where the coffins were kept for display purposes, and out into a carpeted hall. We went for the big stair case, side by side.

"Let me go first," I suggested.

If he liked to look at a woman, I'd give him the opportunity. I skipped in front of him, went up the treads. He was below me, he had a perfect view of my rounded buttocks, the backs of my curving thighs. He could even see the hairs at my crotch as I moved one slim leg and then the other, mounting the staircase.

I heard him panting like a creaky bellows.

A little more than halfway up the stairs he caught my bare hips in his arms and buried his flushed face in my behind, kissing the soft flesh. He acted like a schoolboy, or a man long away from feminine companionship. Well, maybe he had been away from womenfolk a long time, for all I knew. If he had a fetish about womenfolk and clothes, could be he didn't get much of an opportunity for giving it full play. Well, that was why I was here getting my behind kissed. I had to make him need my special branch of sex play so much he'd take me with him when he went to pick up that gadget from his Sicilian bosses.

His tongue licked across my buttockflesh.

His voice whispered words in Italian. Now I can talk Italian with the best of them, but my backside so close to his lips interfered with his enunciation so I couldn't make out what it was he said. But I took it for an indication that he was having a ball.

I wriggled my fanny in his face, rubbing it back and forth. "Go on, honey," I pleaded. "Don't stop. You sure know how to make a girl feel good. I go for you, I really do."

He rumbled laughter, kissing my buttocks again, but as if saying farewell to them for a little while. "Here I'm keepin' you standin' here, and we got all those clothes to put you in."

"Well, let's go, then," I carolled. I turned and shook a finger at him merrily. "You have a groovy way of distracting a girl, honeybear. How do you expect me to pay attention to what you want when you're loving my rearend?"

He stared up at me with his black eyes, cowlike in his delight at my performance. I mentally hugged myself. My game plan was still on the tracks and roaring along at express speed. I bent and let my hand slide down his front, across his neatly striped trousers. I'd have bet a cookie any other girl friends he'd had here had been interested only in the money they were going to get, not in showing Joe baby a good time. He acted like it, anyhow. Me, I enjoy my work. My fingertips encountered something like a big bone shoving up against his pants leg. His eyes got glassy as my fingers went up and down that erection.

"Is this what I think it is?" I cooed.

He swallowed, nodding. He was sweating a lot, now.

"We're going to have fun with this, aren't we?"

My hand wrapped about his elongated penis. I squeezed it a couple of times while his open mouth made choking sounds. Then I let him go, whirled and ran for the top of the stairs.

He stood a moment, tottering on the tread where he was standing, mouth open and eyes half closed. I heard him cry out, "Never have I met a girl like you. Never! It will not be easy to . . . leave you. . . ."

"Then don't," I told him, turning on the landing, lifting my arms on either side of my head with my legs spread slightly.

His eyes devoured my nudity, starting at my ankles and going up my curving calves to my dimpled knees and then to my full thighs. They zeroed in on my bushy mons veneris, held for several moments—I told myself he could see the red clitoral bud jutting from between my genital folds—before sliding up to my belly. When his stare finally got around to my breasts, I gave my shoulders a little shake.

My eyes didn't need the hall mirror in which I was reflected to know that my tits were doing a jiggle and bounce. My nipples went up and down and sideways as my breasts jerked only slightly, they were so hard and swollen. My ribs could be seen, if Joe baby wanted to count their ridges against my pink flesh, and then my moving belly. I couldn't see my thatch of red pubic hair in the mirror, but the man below me could.

"Marrone," he whispered.

"Where are those clothes?" I challenged.

"Never mind the clothes!" he sobbed, starting up the stairs.

"Oh, yes," I cried. "You got them because you wanted to see me in them. I want to put them on for you. Besides, it will make you even stronger—the waiting."

He nodded blankly, stumbling on the carpeted treads. I backed away from him on bare feet, waiting for him to show me the way into the bedroom. I figured he wanted it that way, it was part of his hangup about clothes and women. I wondered what quirk had directed his sexual energies to this voyeuristic end.

Discovering this was no part of my job, so I let

him slide his arm about me without asking questions, and walked as he did toward a partly opened door. His right arm lifted, his hand pushed open the wooden door.

I was staring into a room filled with mirrors.

There were mirrors on the walls, the ceiling was a number of mirrors cunningly joined together and even the floor was of reflecting glass. I made the proper sounds, oohing and aahing as I stood on the threshold.

This boy really liked to see what he was doing with a dame!

He waited for my reaction, not breathing. Maybe some girls in the past, to whom he'd showed this little sex sanctuary of his, had rebelled at this part of it. A lot of women don't like to be watched while they're making love or being made love to. Me, I'm different. I like sex any way, which way.

I ran into the room. I was a hundred girls, all at once. My naked body was framed in the ceiling, on the walls, even on the floor. I threw my arms wide, I did a bump and grind, watching my breasts leap and shake.

Joe Turessi sobbed, staring at me. "The clothes," he panted. "The clothes. Put them on. You gotta!"

"Where are they?"

The only things in the room outside of my naked bod were a bureau and a low bed, king size, seemingly without footboards or headboards. The bed had them, but they were hidden by a black satin counterpane. That black satin would show off my nudity to this man the way a rare pearl is displayed on an ebon velvet pad.

Joe baby ran across the room, opened a mirrored door. I could see evening gowns, sport clothes, knitted jerseys, jump suits and hot pants, all the paraphernalia that makes the female attractive to the male.

"Why, honeybear?" I wondered out loud. "Or shouldn't I ask?"

His eyes ate into mine. "I'll tell—you. I wouldn't tell nobody else. But there's somethin' about you that makes me know you'd understand. You're not like the other holes I've had. You're special, kid. But first you gotta get into them clothes."

He ran to the only other article of furniture in the room besides the bed. He opened a drawer and drew out a pair of black nylons and a lacey garterbelt. He tossed them to me, telling me to put them on.

"Sit on the bed," he whispered, face flushed.

So I plunked my buttocks down on the edge of the black satin counterpane and took the nylons out of the package. They were brand new, so was the garterbelt in its paper receptacle. I rolled the stocking up, wriggled my pink toes so he'd see they were painted red to match my hair, then slid them into the nylon. Up my shapely leg I rolled the nylon slowly while Joe stood there goggling, eating my inner thighs and my exposed crotch with his hard black eyes.

"I was brought up in a crummy neighborhood, ya know?" he began. "I was the only boy inna family. I had two sisters and my mother. She was young, then, and pretty. My sisters were pretty, too. My room—well, it wasn't very big, just about room for a bed. But there was a crack in the plaster between my room and theirs. Jeez! It's hell to be poor, kid. I know. Alla time I was growin' up, I used to lie there inna dark and peek into the next room an' watch my sisters getting undressed for bed or dressed to go out."

His face lost its dreamy look, grew hard as he glanced at me. "I never shot my mouth off like this before, ya know? You tell anybody about this and. . . ."

There was no need for him to say any more. He'd give a contract on me so a hit man would make sure I left the land of the living. Maybe my face got white, because he chuckled suddenly, nodding. "Don't mind me, kid. I'm suspicious of everybody."

I waited patiently. As a member of the N.Y.M.P.H.O. family, I am well versed in many subjects, psychology being one of them. What had happened to little Joey Turessi was not so unusual. He'd been exposed to the female bodies of his sisters and his mother at an early age, maybe his libido always remembered them and needed something to put him in mind of them whenever he wanted sex. It happens all the time, but he was uptight about it, feeling guilt associations. He probably even had youthful erections, seeing female nudity for the first time. And so his fetish was fixed for him even before he knew about such things.

"First time I ever had a woman, I was a flop. Couldn't get it up. I felt crummy, thought maybe I wasn't a man. You know, impotent. Then one night years later I asked a woman I knew to take her clothes off for me. I promised her some money. She did what I asked and—*marrone*! I was up like a bull in rut. Sure I tumbled the dame, she expected it for all the bread I promised her. And my eyes were open."

All during the time he'd been talking I'd been putting on the stockings. Now with both of them on my legs, slightly crumpled at my thighs as I stood, I reached for the garterbelt and drew it around my middle. Joe baby ate me with his eyes. I bent over so my heavy breasts dangled between my arms and did up the stocking vamps to the garters.

"After that," he went on saying, "I knew what to do when I hadda dame. Before I had her, I made her undress. But this got borin', so I had her get dressed. This gave me the hots, too. After a time I realized that what was givin' me the greatest satisfaction was to see a dame in different clothes, like they was my sisters or my mother puttin' on their different dresses.

"I was okay, after that. Hell, I couldn't tell this to

nobody. Every *capo* in the outfit would laugh at me if it got out. So I had to be careful, you know? Like havin' you here now. The *rapparesente*—the big boss —wouldn't like to know I hadda get my kicks that way, see? I'm a *capo* myself, a lieutenant, and I don't want to lose my place in the structure. That's why I had to sneak you in."

I decided to take his mind off himself and fasten it on me.

I stood and pirouetted in front of him. My reflection leaped into motion on ail sides. My nyloned legs were smoothly curved columns, my pale thighs above were pillars of sexuality and my plumply mounded buttocks framed by the garterbelt across my middle were invitations to venery.

There were evening shoes near the bed, rhine-stoned Kimels. I pushed my feet into them and hip-swung a path across the mirrored floor toward my host. I put fingers to his coat, slid it off. I undid his tie, unfastened his shirt buttons. In seconds, I had him down to his Fruit of the Loom boxer shorts. His erection was up away from his front, jutting out like Omar the Tentmaker.

I slid my nails along that flesh-bar.

"I could be all women to you, honey," I breathed, letting my hard nipples slide across his hairy chest. "What with wigs and makeup I could make myself into any number of females."

I felt it was about time to make my pitch. After

all, I do work for N.Y.M.P.H.O., and my job was to get myself invited to Europe with this man, to find out what the Mafia big bosses had in mind for him and stop them, if I could. I was working in the dark, but I'm quick-witted enough to roll with the punches and change my tactics when I see how the wind is blowing.

He didn't say a word, which I took as a good sign, so I let my hand slide under the outthrust shorts and run gently along his rearing manhood. Joe Turessi moaned and his eyes had a faraway look.

I thought I could read the signs; he was reliving something out of his boyhood past. I whispered, "Who am I, Joe, honey?"

"A woman. After a party at our place. She was. . . ."

". . . wearing an evening gown?"

He nodded, shaking. "A cheap one. But still. . . ."

"Go get it for me, darling."

Now my father is a doctor; a psychiatrist, to be exact. As a child I'd read his medical books, his tomes by Stekel, Freud, Jung and Adler. I thought I understood Joe Turessi perhaps better than he knew himself. He was a voyeur, certainly, but he was something more than this, he was also a bit of a masochist.

I'd have bet a cookie that he had a touch of the Oedipus complex brush as well. He had seen his mother in that room, getting undressed or in a nightgown or maybe naked, half a hundred times. He'd watched her roll on her stockings, watched her get dressed. Deep down in his psyche, so far down he never even thought about it, he had a thing about his mom. I'd bet she was at the bottom of his hang-ups.

It was too early to go for broke with him, though. I held my breath while his eyes cleared and he looked at me. "Get the evening gown for you?"

"Please, darling? You pick it out."

An unholy glee came into his face. "Yeah," he breathed. "Yeah, I'll go get it for you."

He almost ran to the closet, hunted among the gorgeous dresses hanging there. He turned and I saw a black satin evening gown, lowcut at the breast and without any back at all, to speak of. His hands trembled as they touched it.

I decided to risk it. "What was your mother like, honeybear?

He was still in the grip of feverish desire and of that youthful memory to which he clung unwittingly at such times. "She was a lot like you. Beautiful. Young. But with brown hair not red like yours. Her breasts. . . ."

His eyes touched my swollen titties. He sobbed and shook his head. He could not go on talking about it, so I didn't press him. I knew enough.

He brought me the dress, a Givenchy. His mother had probably never heard of Givenchy. I took it from him and slipped it down over my head. He was very close, so near that the tip of his bloated manhood touched my stockinged thigh. As the skirt of the gown fell, it brushed him there, made him cry out hungrily.

I doubted that he had ever been this close to his mother when she had dressed. I think he had seen her dress or undress from his room, at one time or another, and he'd fantasied—as boys and men will do—on an event which gave him a lot of pleasure.

In other words, he and I were acting out one of his most delightful fantasies. We were not only performing his normal bag, that of merely watching a woman dress and then undress for him. We were on another sexual level: we were in the middle of one of his most precious daydreams.

I could have hugged myself. I was sure that this was the Open Sesame I needed to get him to take me to Europe with him! I had stumbled on the magic key to unlock the secret doorways of his libido. And there is nothing stronger in a man than his libido, believe me. It makes him into a world conqueror or a money tycoon when it's sublimated, it turns him into a Don Juan when he channels it along sexual lines.

I moved back and forth in the evening gown with its rhinestone decorations. I wore no jewelry, that would have added to the illusion he was seeing, of course, but I had no jewelry on me other than my

Piaget wristwatch. I was going to make him need me at his side as much as he needed the air he breathed.

I moved up against him, plastered my front against him, my arms about his neck, and glued my lips and tongue to him. My hips lifted and bumped. I felt his savage erection between my thighs and closed them on its tip. Joe Turessi was sobbing softly even as his arms banded my middle and held me tight.

I let my hands slide down from his neck, along his back to his shorts and inside them to his buttocks; I dug my long red fingernails into his flesh. He grunted, but he was pleased. Then I inched his shorts down until they pooled at his bare feet.

"Lift my skirt, darling," I breathed.

His hands did my bidding until the evening gown was bunched about my slim waist. He pressed closer, my thighs widened; I took his stiff flesh between my soft inner thighs, rubbed it. I had to make his fantasy about his most secret desires come alive. If I failed to do this, I was going to let N.Y.M.P.H.O. down.

Not to mention the danger that might result to my native land and to its honest, law-abiding citizens.

I drew him by the hand toward the bed. I pushed him until he sat on the edge of the black satin counterpane. I stood between his slightly parted legs and lifted the long skirt of the evening gown.

"Kiss mamma," I breathed.

His eyes glazed over. My heart pounded triumphantly. I was right! This man did have an incestuous thing going for his mother. And I was helping him unleash it, letting it all hang out. But only by this method would I be able to bind myself to him so closely that he wouldn't be happy without me somewhere around so I could play Mom to his sexuality.

His mouth roved over my upper thighs, my belly. Those lips buried themselves in my pubic bush. He kissed, I felt his tongue searching amid the hairs for my rigid clitoris. His tonguetip touched it, tapped it, licked.

I did some moaning myself, echoing his own sobbing passions. My hips went back and forth slowly, moving against his mouth and tongue. My fingers twined in his hair.

"Now, darling?" I asked gently.

"Yes, yes. Now. Now, please!"

I turned around, exposing my trembling buttocks to his stare. Then I straddled his legs as he closed them and sat back, parting my labial folds and grasping his bloated manhood. I inched down slowly, hearing him cry out in utter pleasure as I took more and more of him inside me.

I let my buttocks rest on his belly for a moment. My interior muscles—the constrictor cunnae—I put to work, flexing and loosening them as might the fingers of a milkmaid about the teat of a cow. I held

Joe Turessi in the most intense physical pleasure he had ever known, I believe.

Only after a few minutes, when I felt he was ready for it, did I begin to rise and fall, very slowly, very lazily, on his sex shaft buried to his balls in my genital tunnel. He was sobbing, cursing softly under his breath. His hips rose and fell, his manhood surged up and fell away. He pumped at me savagely, then tenderly.

His hands were going over my hips caressingly. Those hands lifted to slide under my armpits and around in front to where my naked breasts were bobbing gently to my posting motions. Feet planted firmly on the mirrored floor, I was going up and down; back and forth, while the sound of our moist flesh meeting made an exciting sound in the room.

"Honeybear," I whispered.

"Mmmmm?"

"You're the most potent man I've ever met. I wish. . . ."

I let my words fade, hang in the air between us.

"Wha—whadda ya wish?"

"I wish this was more than just a one-time stand."

"Oh, yeah . . . me, too."

My hips moved more rapidly. I didn't say anything more, I wanted him to think about what I'd said, to reflect on it. He had to believe the idea of taking me with him to Europe was his own, not mine. Meanwhile, I must set myself to making him need me all the more.

I rose up away from him. He yelled in fury at being deprived of his pleasure, but I lifted off the evening gown and sent it flying with a flip of my hand and wrist. He had been lying back on the bed, his legs bent at the knees and dangling over its edge. Now he raised up on his elbows and stared at my nakedness in the garterbelt and black nylons.

"I wanted to be naked too, darling," I smiled.

Understanding burst in him. His erection, covered with my secretions, glistening like a greased totem pole and jutting upward from his loins, was almost about to burst, too. He lay back, waiting.

"Okay, okay. But—h-hurry," he panted.

I got on my hands and knees above him. My breasts hung down inches from his lips. I dipped my left shoulder so that my left breast slid across his mouth. His lips parted, drew me in.

He nursed hungrily, like an infant. I fed him my other breast. Then, while he was still sucking, I lowered my hips to capture him again inside me. In this woman-above position, I could control the action, and did. I rammed up and down on him, I slowed the action until my hips were barely moving. Then I circled them, as though I had a hula hoop about my middle.

I was staring down into his contorted face.

I saw his eyes roll back, his body stiffen. His mouth jerked convulsively, spittle came to the corners of his mouth. He jerked and jerked and went limp.

"Joey, what's wrong?" I whispered, terrified.

He didn't answer me. How could he? He was dead.

Chapter Two

I froze there for about one whole minute. One minute is a long time, if you measure it on a watch. My brain was numb, I was crying inside me. The man who was to take me to Europe as an Uncle Sam agent unbeknownst to him, lay white and still beneath me. I had killed him.

Cherry Delight had struck again!

The only thing was, I hadn't meant to kill him. It wasn't part of the plan. He had to be alive, to take me to wherever it was he was going to meet the higher-ups in his Mafia family. Without him, I was a failure.

I scrambled off him, heart thudding wildly. Maybe he wasn't dead, maybe he'd just fainted. I grabbed his wrist, felt his pulse. None. I bent over his chest, listening to his heartbeat. No heartbeat, either. And when I put a mirror to his lips, there was not the faintest bit of moisture on the glass.

Oh, Joe Turessi was dead, all right. And I'd killed him.

I sat on the edge of the bed and wanted to cry. Damn! It had been in the bag. He had been ripe to take me to Europe with him. I knew it, my female intuition told me as much. I had ways of pleasing him. No other dame did. And now—this!

My common sense realized he'd had a heart attack, a massive thrombosis. A fat lot of good that knowledge did me. Wearily I rose from the bed, moved to pick up the black satin evening gown and carry it to the closet.

I paused, staring at those garments on their hangers.

They all looked brand new. I wondered for a second if Joe Turessi had bought them especially for me. My fellow workers at N.Y.M.P.H.O. had learned that the Mafia man had a thing for seeing girls dressing and then undressing. They'd wangled an order from him for a visit from a Femme Fatale: me. And N.Y.M.P.H.O. had counted on my going to Europe with Turessi.

Well, it was a cinch I couldn't go with him. But— could I go without him?

On my own. With his consent. No, better than that: by his orders. I glanced over my shoulder at his dead body. Hmmmm, I'd have to do something about that corpse. Still, with a number of empty coffins in the storage chamber, that shouldn't be too in-surmountable a problem.

I ran downstairs in my black nylons and garter-belt. Hell, it was after hours, it must have been thirty minutes past midnight. The mortuary was in dark-ness outside the mirrored room. I fumbled around until I found a light switch.

Then I went hunting for his office. It was a wood-paneled room, outfitted with a big mahogany desk and swivel chair, with sombre files recessed behind heavy green drapes, a mantlepiece and fireplace where once logs had burned when this building had been a private home. There was a typewriter on a stand, covered.

I found typing paper in the desk, drew the Rem-ington a little closer, and started to bang the keys. I wrote a nice letter introducing me to the man our International Intelligence unit assured us was named Benito Castracia. His title in the Mob was that of Coordinator, which meant he might be the bossman of the entire Mafia empire.

It took me half an hour to phrase the thing prop-erly. When I was done I had a neatly typed missive. It needed a forged signature. I let my rhinestoned evening pumps take me upstairs so I could examine the articles in Joe Turessi's discarded clothes where they lay on the mirrored floor. I found a driving li-cense with his signature. I practiced it about twenty times before I scrawled it across the bottom of the letter.

I folded the letter and stared at it. What do I do now? I asked myself. I had no money, not even a handbag. Still. . . .

Joe Turessi would have money. He was ready to take a jet from Kennedy to Paris. He needed spending money. There had been a hundred clams in the wallet from which I'd borrowed his driving license. This meant he had some bread stashed away somewhere else. The funeral parlor safe? It seemed a safe bet, no pun meant.

I have been trained by experts to open safes, at least of the wall variety represented by the old-fashioned one that was hidden by a bit of that same green drapery that kept the filing cabinets out of sight. It took only ten minutes to find the combo.

There was three thousand iron men in the safe, plus his airline ticket on an Air France jet to Paris, another ticket for a subsidiary line to fly him south to Nice. From Nice, he would travel by rented car to Saint Tropez. When he arrived in Saint Tropez, there were reservations for him at the Byblos Hotel. What Joe Turessi could do, so could I.

The name J. Turessi was scrawled on all the tickets, the reservations. I would become Josefina Turessi. Time enough to worry about his fellow Mafia men when I was safely inside the Byblos.

I ran upstairs, selected an A-line dress and slipped into it. There were no brassieres available, evidently

Joe baby had liked to see breasts jiggle. So for the nonce, I'd be a member of Women's Lib. I settled on the St. Lafrent skirt—it was not quite a mini but it was short enough—about my nyloned legs and fluffed my hair into some semblance of a coiffure. The many mirrors told me I was a real sexpot.

Then I started gathering underthings, spare stockings and such, and stuffing them into the two Tourister valises stamped with the initials I.T. I folded dresses and a couple of sheer nighties into the same bags. Joe baby had bought these clothes with an eye to their sexuality, and since I had the right kind of body to fill them out, I knew I was going to cause some raised eyebrows to Saint Tropez.

My Piaget wristwatch told me I had plenty of time to make the nine ayem jetliner to Paris. It was around four in the morning, now. But I was ready to travel.

I lifted the dead body onto my shoulder in a fireman's hitch and staggered toward and down the mortuary stairs. I had to stop and rest every so often, Joe Turcssi had not been a fat man, but he sure was a dead weight right about now. Finally I got him into a coffin and closed the lid, wondering how long it would take somebody to find him.

I ran back for the Tourister bags, carried them down the stairs and out onto the parking lot. My eyes touched a Ford Galaxie. I had car keys in my hand that I'd taken, along with his money and airplane tickets, from the dead man. I was betting those keys fitted the Galaxie ignition slot.

They did. Ten minutes later I was wheeling along a highway en route to Kennedy International Airport. A few miles from the turn-off I swung onto a side street and cruised around until I found a public telephone.

I dialed Mark Condon's number.

His sleepy voice answered me, but when I told him what had happened, he wasn't sleepy any more. There was a pregnant silence. Then:

"You can't go off by yourself, Cherry, you'll be sticking your pretty neck in the lion's mouth."

"I have to, Mark. It's the only way we can find out why Turner was to fly to the Riviera and what the Sicilian crowd wants with him. I'm posing as one of his operatives. I'm hoping the Mafia big brass will believe me."

"All they have to do is make a transoceanic telephone call to learn Turessi's dead. Then what do they do with you?"

"Don't remind me. It's a risk I've got to take. We may never get another chance like this."

"I'm going to call the Controller. There's no reason why he should be getting a good night's sleep while we worry about the state of national security."

"Just don't let him interfere."

"I don't like it. You're taking on more than you can chew."

"I have strong teeth. Besides, this is as good a chance as any to let the upper echelon crowd know what I can do on my own."

"You're a newcomer to our organization. You may not have enough training."

"Who has, for this kind of case?"

"All right, all right. But I'm going to phone the bossman."

"Wait until eight o'clock. Tell him I phoned you just before takeoff. Will you do this for me, Mark?"

Usually Mark Condon is a very hardheaded case officer. He is my contact with the Controller, I take my orders from him. But Mark Condon knew just as well as I did that this was a one-in-a-million opportunity that might not come again.

"Okay, okay. But be careful."

I hung up and ran for the Galaxie before he could change his mind. I drove at sixty miles per hour until I was at Kennedy, searching the lettered signs for the Air France pavilion. It was getting lighter in the western sky, pretty soon it would be dawn. I was early, but I figured to check in my bags and find a place to eat before they started calling flight time.

Everything went nicely. The girl clerk at the Air France desk was not suspicious. After all, J. Turessi could very well be Josefina Turessi. She stamped my ticket, attached markers on the Tourister bags, then handed me back my tickets. She did seem a little surprised that I didn't have a handbag, and her plucked brows rose upward.

I flashed her a sweet smile and beat feet.

Nobody knew any better than I that I needed a handbag, some sort of gadget to stow away the wallet, car keys, and other assorted objects a woman needs that reposed now in the pocket of the one coat Joe baby had bought for his lady to wear. It was a fun-fur thing and looked absolutely hideous. I planned to ditch it as soon as I could and buy myself a new one.

I dozed a little in the big waiting room until about six-thirty. All the time I catnapped, I did so with one eye open, because I wouldn't have put it past Mark Condon and the Controller to come racing in through the glass doors and carry me back to my city pad telling me to forget the whole thing. Maybe Mark did some hot arguing, or maybe he did what I asked, didn't call until eight o'clock, because nobody showed.

I ate in the terminal grille and found a store open where I could pick up a fringed shoulder bag. It didn't go too well with my St. Laurent A-line, but it held all the things I crammed into it.

Naturally, I would much rather have had a couple of weapons in that bag, say a snub-nosed revolver and a little gas-gun or two, but beggars definitely can't have their druthers. Unarmed but filled with ham and scrambled eggs, toast and coffee, I headed for the boarding ramp.

At eight-fifteen, the Air France jet went down its runway and up into the blue morning sky. I lay my head against the pillow and closed my eyes. The seat-belt had me secure, nobody was going to cancel my flight at this late date, so I felt I could relax.

I slept for a few hours. Then it was time for lunch, so a stewardess in an Air France blue cap and dress woke me. I feasted on braised boeuf a la mode, salad, and a chocolate souffle served with hot coffee, curled up and went back to sleep.

We descended through clouds and a squalling rainstorm onto Orly Field in darkness. A little checking with the stewardess told me I'd have an hour's wait before another plane would pick me up and deposit me in Nice.

This would give me the chance to change my American dollars into French francs. Even at the present rate of exchange, I'd get a lot of new francs for a thousand of those iron men. Hell, the money wasn't mine. What did I care if I couldn't buy as much in France as I could in Uncle Sam land for them? I was here as a guest of Giuseppi Turessi, whose money was tucked neatly inside my fringed shoulder bag.

I would have dearly loved to do a little shopping in Paris, being a female sort of girl who loves fine clothes and other assorted goodies, but this would have to wait. I marched myself to a branch of the national bank and tendered a night-time teller a thousand American bucks. I got back a lot of new francs, and stuffed them into my bag.

As I was turning away, a man said softly, *"S'il vous plait, vous serez bien servi. Un monseiur veut vous voir."*

The man was telling me he wanted to serve me, and that a man wanted to see me. He didn't pause, he'd spoken out of the corner of his mouth, almost inaudibly so only I could hear him. I did a right face and trotted off at a little distance behind him.

He was well dressed, he might have been a lawyer or some sort of professional man. My hunch was he worked for N.Y.M.P.H.O. He halted near a door and lighted a Galoise.

I came to a stop near him, fiddled in my shoulder bag. "You wanted to see me?"

"You'ave come to go to Saint Tropez, no? You are from the New York Mafia Prosecution and Harassment Organization, no?"

"Right on both counts, dad. What gives?"

"There will be a third piece of luggage waiting for you at Nice. It contains what you may need. And m'sieu le controller says to be goddam careful."

He drew a deep puff from the Galoise, blew out the smoke slowly as though savoring it, and walked away. I found I had no compact in my bag, made a moué of displeasure, and marched to a *pharmacie* where I bought a lipstick and an Estee Lauder compact.

Thus reinforced, I went to board the jetliner. Everything went off smooth as cream, at first. The jet landed, I disembarked and marched into the airline terminal to retrieve my luggage. But as I put my hands on the handles, two beefy men with hard eyes came up on either side of me.

"You are not Joseph Turessi," one of them said.

"What are you doing with his luggage?" the other asked.

I smiled brightly. "Well, of course I'm not Joseph Turessi. I'm here in his place. Joe baby couldn't come."

The man blinked. They were what is known as buttons. In other words, they were the lowest in the Mafia scale, the workers, the goons, the muscle boys. They did not think, they just took orders and carried them out, no matter who got hurt.

My hand gestured at the bags. They bent and lifted them easily in their hamlike hands. Then we stood there for a few seconds while they stared at me.

So I said, "Well, let's get a move on. Take me to your leader."

"The *capo* didn't say anything about a dame."

I sighed. "Joe said I might have trouble. But he gave me a letter to hand to your *capo* or even to your head man, the *rappresente*, if he's around."

They blinked in unison, then they looked at each other. One of them shrugged, as if to say that he didn't know what to do with me so they might as well take me to somebody who did. I went on smiling like a child anxious to please.

Apparently we were going to stand there all day because neither one knew what to do with me and neither wanted to assume the responsibility. If I was ever going to get this show on the road, it was up to me. So I turned on a heel and began walking.

"I have a rented car waiting for me," I called over my shoulder.

"Plans have been changed," said a button.

They guided me toward a waiting black Mercedes-Benz. I walked between them with my heart pounding a little faster than normal because, while I told myself a bold face was the best face to put on at a time like this, their attitude was a threatening one. It told me I was going to have to prove myself.

The ride in the black car was a silent one. We went by way of lonely coastal roads between stone fences and rows of twisted pines that must have been here at the time of the Crusaders. It is an old land, this Provence, and a lovely one with its little walled-in farmhouses called *mas*, and the olive trees shading the little hillsides, beside great vines hung on frames. It was a peaceful scene, something out of a Van Gogh painting.

The Mercedes-Benz swung down toward the sea after a time, heading for a little town where the houses seemed to grow row on row, one a little higher than the other, like huge stepping stones.

They were built of sun-faded brick and stucco and each one boasted pink tile rooftops. They formed a maze to my eyes, kept apart by narrow little alleys and cul-de-sacs. I could see the Mediterranean from here, a boat or two moving across its placid surface, and rows of fishermen's smacks drawn up on a pebbly beach.

Somewhere in among the houses, in front of a narrow building with awnings and an upper balcony, the car braked to a stop. One of the beefy men grunted at me so I got out of the car and stretched, taking in the cobbled street, the houses side by side with one another so that they looked like twins. The air was fragrant with salt, and cool.

"Inside," said the beefiest of the duo.

He opened a street door for me and I walked into cool darkness where the smell of cooking seafood came to meet me. The hall was paneled in wood, there was carpeting on the floor and a staircase to the left. A hand indicated I was to mount the staircase.

Two men were waiting in an upstairs room at the rear of the house that overlooked a little garden where an orange tree was growing. They sat behind two desks, like twin presidents of some big American corporation, dressed in Pierre Cardin suits and wearing ties designed by Christian Dior. They were neat, impeccably dressed, and much more sophisticated than the two bullyboys who'd come to the airport to fetch me.

One man was dark, with blue jowls and a craggy, tough look about him, despite his clothes. His eyes were hard, emotionless as black marbles. His big hands, their backs covered with hair, lay unmoving on the desktop. I would get no sympathy, no understanding from him, my female intuition told me.

The second man was blonde, I felt he came from northern Italy where the golden-haired Vandals had left their mark, centuries ago. His eyes were blue as the Mediterranean sky, he wore his hair long, and neatly coiffed, and there was a shaggy, handlebar moustache framing his rather full lips. He even gave me a smile.

I decided to focus on him. "Hi," I exclaimed lightly, teetering a little so he'd see I didn't have a bra on. "Joe baby sent me."

The blonde one smiled faintly. The other just scowled.

"Joe Turessi," I went on bravely. "You know. Giuseppi Turessi, he's a *capo* in the Outfit."

"And what are you in the outfit?" asked the dark guy.

"I'm Joe's deputy. An *amico nostra*." I sighed. "He told me I'd have trouble, convincing you. He said you'd be very suspicious. I said you might be suspicious, but you wouldn't be stupid. Right?"

"I don't like it," the dark one said in Italian, which I understand very well indeed, having learned it from my father. My mother is Irish, that's where I get my red hair.

In Italian as fluent as his own, I caroled, "I don't blame you." They looked surprised at my knowledge of their language. "In your boots I wouldn't be too happy, either. But it was me go or nobody. Joe's having trouble."

"What kind of trouble?" snapped the blonde.

"His phone is bugged. He thinks the narc boys are on his tail. You know, the narcotics gang, the Treasury Department. He said if he went, it would make them suspicious. So he sent me in his place.

"As a matter of fact, I have a letter from him. May I show it to you?"

Blue-jowls nodded and held out a hairlike paw. I dug the forged letter out of my fringed handbag and handed it over. He read it twice, slowly, then handed it to the blonde. When the blonde had read it, he gave me a faint smile.

"It seems in order. Just the same, we must be absolutely certain you are who you say you are. *Capisce?*"

I knew I was in for it, with these two. They had been expecting Joe Turessi, and by God and His angels, they were going to know why Joe Turessi wasn't here and why I was. My explanation might satisfy them, I blessed my foresight in writing that letter, but for a time I was going to walk on tenterhooks.

I shrugged, "If you want to risk that bug, you can call Joe up. He'll vouch for me."

Now while the mortuary was bugged, even my organization could not prevent the news of Joe Turessi's death from leaking out. Sooner or later, somebody was going to tell blue-jowls and blondie that I was an imposter. I crossed mental fingers in the hope that I'd get what I was after and get a chance to execute the Mafia head man before my cover broke.

I tried not to show how nervous I was. Visions of being tortured ran through my head like sugar plums at Christmastime. Once they were through torturing me they'd put a cyanide pellet in me and feed me to the Mediterranean fish.

Yeccch!

The blonde man said, gesturing at his companion. "This is Francesco Galuppo. I'm Bocca Carducci."

"Me, I'm Cherry Delight."

The blue eyes widened as a grin struggled with those full lips. "What's that you say? Cherry Delight? That's a name?"

"Well, sort of a nickname. My real moniker is Cherise Dellissio."

The dark one, whose name was Francesco Galuppo, said hoarsely, "One thing, Miss Dellissio. Have you any objections to being our guest for—oh, say about a week or so? We must wait for the—ah— shipment, before we can turn it over to you."

"Whatever you say. You're the bosses."

"Good. Oh, one more thing, then you can unpack. We may send one of our men to the United States, a man who knows Joe Turessi well. He will speak with him, learn from him if he sent you here in his place. If he has, there's been no harm done, eh? If he didn't. . . ."

He let his voice trail off while danger for little old me leaped into his black eyes. I would die if his emissary didn't find Joe Turessi and get his stamp of approval for Cherry Delight. Which was an impossibility of course, Joe baby being stone cold dead.

I had about four, maybe five days until then.

Bocca Carduccio smiled at me. "There's to be a party this evening at the Villa Fouquet, where the Countess Colette De Vaux lives." His eyes got a faraway look. "The Countess is very partial to strangers, she made us welcome with both arms when we arrived. She will be delighted to see you and make your acquaintance. You will go with us, of course?"

"How could I refuse?" I asked sweetly.

"She is the daughter of a French *comte*," Frankie boy told me. "Her title is an empty one, France having no more nobility today than the United States of America. Still, here in lower Provence, one indulges petty whims like this, eh?"

His hand reached out, touched a bell. Almost instantly—she must have been waiting in the hall just beyond the door—a pretty girl in the black and white lace uniform of a maid came in.

"Donna will see you to your rooms. For the moment, then, we say farewell." His head made a slight bow. I nodded and turned toward the door.

The maid gave me a brief, almost frightened smile, then wheeled and half ran out into the hall. When I came to join her, she said. "They have taken your bags upstairs. Will you be good enough to follow me?"

Donna was a brunette, built on that lush Italian style of female body which is my own, with heavy breasts and rounded hips and all the other necessary curves that make men drool. Her legs were columns of shapely flesh under the short uniform skirt as she trotted up the stairs ahead of me. From her thighs, I eyed her buttocks that wobbled sweetly to her every stride.

She helped me unpack my things. It didn't take an expert to see that my dresses and such had been disturbed, and not by female hands. Over the open Tourister, Donna and I stared at each other, as females and not as Italian and American.

"These men," she sighed. "Always they are so clumsy."

I was dying of curiosity to examine the contents of that third bag which had joined my luggage at Orly Field, according to the agent who'd talked to me. Now my organization wasn't concerned enough about its female agents to care whether they wore the latest Yves St. Laurent or Givenchy creations. Those agents had put weapons in the number three Tourister. And disguised them as well, I hoped.

Bocca Carducci and Francesco Galuppo had kept me downstairs answering questions, while somebody had gone through my three bags. My heart felt like lead in my ribcage. If that agent in Paris had smuggled me some weapons, I felt sure the Mafia boys would have spotted them by this time.

My hands trembled when I lifted the last bag and threw it on the bed. What was I going to find? I undid the snaps, lifted the lid.

There were a couple of French dresses.

And quite a bit of body jewelry. Gold chains, links, medallions looped together here and there. The most prominent article in the bag was what the Decadent Chic call a bullet belt. No, no, not the kind Wyatt Earp or Wild Bill Hickok carried. This was a body belt of metal to which are fastened brass cartridges, big ones like for a .30-30 rifle. There was also a matching necklet.

Now these bullet belts are a mild smash in socialite circles in Little Old New York and wherever the haute monde gets together. The authorities have clamped down on them, telling their makers not to use live cartridges but make-believe. Otherwise a girl could carry enough ammo on her for a mild guerrilla war.

Still, I had the feeling that these might be dummy dummies, if you follow me. They weren't real bullets, but one or two of them must be *some* kind of weapon. I was anxious to test them, but I couldn't do it with Donna looking on. What struck me as odd was the fact that the Mafia men, since they'd examined the contents of my suitcases, had let such an obvious hiding place for lethal weaponry go unremarked.

Maybe they were just biding their time.

Or—they might have substituted a harmless bullet for the real gadget. I was going to walk on eggs for a little while, I could see that. All this time, I'd kept my features in a poker face. Thoughts were exploding in my head like an active volcano, but you'd never have known it by looking at me.

When the dresses were hung and my undergarments and stockings and body jewelry put away, Donna wanted to know if there was anything else she could do for me. I shook my head and smiled a no-no.

"I'm tired," I explained. "I've been traveling for the past ten hours or so, and I need some shut-eye, if I'm to be at my best tonight for that party."

There is a time differential that seasoned plane travelers encounter which disturbs what is known to the cognoscenti as our circadian rhythms. In other words, the biological timekeeping of our bodies goes into a freak-out because we travel across different time zones when we travel by jetliner these days, that results in a weakening of our thinking processes.

When Donna went out and closed the door behind her, I dropped across the big bed and just lay there. I had things to do: I wanted to search the room for bugs, maybe even a television camera or a one-way mirror, but all that could wait. I needed to be at my most alert to do any searching.

A knock sounded on the door.

"Come on in," I called, expecting Donna with some towels, maybe.

Bocca Carducci opened the door. His blue eyes got a little big at the sight of me stretched out on the bed. An apologetic smile came to his lips.

"I am sorry to disturb you. I just wanted to let you know that we decided to put through a transatlantic phone call to Joe Turessi."

I died the death, right there.

"He was most profuse in his apologies for not having been able to come over himself," the big blonde man went on. "He vouches for you, says you are an American citizen who's been working with him as part of his family. He trusts you, he says you're very clever. I thought you might want to know."

He smiled, bowed, and went out of the room.

I told myself I was going crazy.

Or maybe—dreaming!

Chapter Three

I was asleep. I had to be! Otherwise, the big blonde man would never have told me he'd been talking to Joe Turessi. Joe Turessi was dead. Complete. My hands had verified that, had even put him in the coffin.

"It's a damn good thing you're lying on a bed, Cherry Delight," I told myself. "Otherwise you'd have fallen down in a faint."

As it was, I could hardly move.

Now either Bocca Carducci had lied or someone had faked Joe baby's voice. I didn't see how this last could be, because the organization boys didn't dare move in on the Mafia mortuary. Not, at least, until we had them dead to rights where we could make arrests and make them stick in court. My mind went full circle and came around to the inescapable fact: blonde boy had lied through his teeth.

To see how I would react? Maybe. If I'd betrayed myself, he would have known it by a blink of an eyelash, the sudden whiteness of my face, a gasp. Maybe that disturbance of my circadian rhythms was standing me in good stead. I'd been too time-punchy to show any reaction.

I let my eyelids close. . . .

A hand woke me, shaking my shoulder. My eyelids went up, I saw Donna and Bocca Carducci staring down at me. They looked worried.

"Whazzit?" I mumbled. God! I must look a fright.

"We were worried," said Donna. "You were so still, so quiet."

"We thought. . . ."

"What did you think, Bocca?" I asked sweetly.

His eyes were wary. "You looked so still, I was afraid you'd taken poison."

"Poison?" I shrieked. "Why in hell should I take poison?"

I sat up, sending my short skirthem flying above my garterclasps and showing some of my soft pink thighflesh. I knew damn well what he'd thought, it was all there in his face for me to read, so I figured I might as well play my indignation to the hilt.

I slid across the bed, making my skirt rise even higher. Bocca got a hungry glare in his blue eyes as the entire length of my nyloned legs and bare thighs came into view. I wore no panties, Joe Turessi hadn't had them in his wardrobe, so he got a better than good look at my curling red pubic hair.

Staring him right in the eye and seeing him flush, I slowly pulled the skirthem down a little. "You don't believe me," I said coldly. "You think I'm an American secret agent of some sort. Is that it? Well, if that's the way you want it to be, so be it. I'll clear out of here right away."

"Please," Bocca said. "Let's not jump to conclusions. You're our guest. I want you to know that."

"Some guest," I groused. "I lie down to take a little nap and everybody thinks I committed suicide. Now why is that? You tell me, please."

"You were so s-still," quavered Donna.

Her eyes held a pleading look. I got the message. She had found me, she's the one who panicked and ran for golden boy. If I made more of a stink, she might get in real trouble.

"Oh, well," I carolled in answer to her silent plea. "There's been no harm done. I guess I sleep like a dead person. Hmmmm. I'm supposed to go to a party tonight, right?"

The maid beamed. "I will help you dress."

The big blonde man grinned. *Eccellente!* We'll have a marvelous time. The Countess gives unforgettable parties."

He ran his eyeballs over me one more time, to make sure he remembered the way my nyloned legs looked, exposed almost to my crotch, and the manner in which my breasts shoved out against the thin material of my dress. Since I wore no bra, they showed pretty clearly, and they shook ripely when I moved.

He left the room a bit reluctantly, I thought.

Donna beamed. "What dress would you like to wear?"

"The black satin evening gown," I told her, with memories of Joe Turessi in mind. "Nothing under it but me and a pair of evening slippers."

I slid off the bed, stood and stretched. "A shower first, then the gown." I bent, caught the hem of the A-line and lifted it off over my head. This left me stark naked except for the garterbelt and nylons.

Donna let her eyes drift over me lazily. Hungrily, too? I felt my nipples get big as she caressed them with her stare. Now I can go AC or DC when it comes to sex, I've made love to women in my job as secret agent for the organization, and been made love to by females. It's a facet of my pudendal personality that endears me to my superiors. My bed-bunny bag, so to speak.

The girl licked her lips. "May I—scrub your back?" she whispered.

"Be my guest, honey."

My fingers went to the garterclasps that held up my Hanes hosiery, but Donna was way ahead of me, on her knees and putting her hands to the snaps. She was very close to my bare thigh, I felt her hot breath. Her fingers lingered at their task of rolling down the nylons—her soft warm palms were caressing my legs as she bared them—and when I lifted each leg for her to remove the stockings, her eyes went up between my legs to my hairy crotch.

When she was done, she pressed a kiss against my inner thighs. She would have done more if she dared, I'm sure. Then she rose and came behind me, unsnapping the garterbelt and tossing it aside. Her hands lay against my hips just for a moment. Almost, they gave me a little squeeze.

"You'd better take off your uniform," I told her. "Or you'll get it all messed up in that shower."

She giggled and yanked off the uniform. She wore black lace panties and a thin bra to match. She was big in the titties, too. Her milky white breasts shook gelatinously as she reached behind her and unfastened the bra. Her nipples were red, the size of half dollars.

Hooking thumbs in the panties, she pushed them off her behind. This left her in just high-heeled French-styled shoes. No clodhoppers for her. She kicked the pumps off and advanced on me.

She didn't stop walking until her bare body bumped mine. Our breasts touched, our bellies mashed and our pubic bushes meshed. "Sorry," she said softly, her black eyes flirting with me. "I didn't mean to bump into you."

The hell you didn't, honey! Still, it was kind of fun, feeling her softness against my own. I reached out, ran my palms down her naked sides. She shivered.

"What about the backscrub?" I laughed.

She walked ahead of me, letting her ass-flesh roll. She had a good body, fleshy but not fat, with all the proper female gadgetry right in the proper place. I wondered if Bocca Carducci knew that Donna was inclined to the Sapphic sisterhood.

Donna put her hand in the shower water, making sure it was the right temperature, before she bade me to get into the glass-enclosed stall. I stepped into the cascade, then slid sideways to give her room. Her hand caught a bar of soap, began lazily to move it all over my back.

It was nice to be waited on this way. I just stood there and let her suds me up, then felt the water flow all over me. She paid especial attention to my buttocks, rubbing her soapy fingers between them, all over the full cheeks, before she turned me so she could clean my front.

My eyes were closed as I felt the soap go over my hardening breasts. With a little cry, as soon as my teats were smothered in scented foam, Donna let the soap fall to the tiled floor and put her hands where the soap was. Back and forth she slid her fingers, gently and caressingly. She worked those suds all over my blue-veined breastflesh until she had each mammary as hard as a rock. I heard myself moaning deep in my throat while my hips were doing a lazy hula.

"Bocca and Francesco are unfeeling pigs," she whispered.

"Compared to you, they are," I breathed.

"I love playing with you this way, holding your tits and shaking them—like this!" She panted as her wetly slick hands went under my breasts and shook them. She didn't shake them very much, they were too hard.

I remembered Mark Condon and the way he'd teased me with that ostrich feather. Was Donna here for the same purpose? Was she getting the mare hot for the stud? What kind of parties did the Countess throw, anyhow? My common sense told me it wouldn't hurt to ask Donna about them. So I did.

"Parties out of a naughty dream," she giggled. rubbing her thumbs over my hard brown nipples, bending them and watching them straighten out. "Anything goes, anything. Oh, you'll have a wonderful time."

Her hands slid down to my belly. She was sobbing softly to herself, licking her full mouth with her tongue. I felt a little sorry for Donna, she was Italian and Italians are supposedly hot-blooded Latins. She was plenty hot-blooded, all right, but she was inclined to lesbianism and the Mafia brotherhood might take a dim view of that.

Her knees buckled and she dropped before me. Now with her eyes on a level with my pubic hair, matted against my mons veneris by soap and water, she began to rub me. Her slick fingers went between my thighs which I widened, and they made sure the soap went everywhere. She had me climbing the shower wall in seconds.

I was a little surprised that she didn't inch closer on her knees and bury her mouth where her hands were fondling me so deliriously. But maybe she had orders to whet my amoral appetites and go only so far. Always assuming I might be receptive to a pussy pitch by a woman, that is.

When she pulled away, I was gasping and jerking. I think there were tears in my eyes, tears of want, but maybe it was only shower drops. At any rate she sat back on her heels and looked up at my nakedness with utter worship in her eyes.

"You aren't going to—stop now?" I choked.

"I must," She swallowed hard. "It is time for you to dress. I must have you ready when they leave for the villa."

I smiled down at her. "Then dry and powder me," I ordered.

She nodded, got to her feet and stepped out of the shower. The towel in her hands became an intimate thing on my breasts and buttocks, on the sensitive lips between my thighs. She had me moaning all over again before she was done. I sure was ready for any sort of bung bash the Countess might have in mind.

The black satin evening gown from Givenchy slithered over my nude curves. It was low cut in front, the inner slopes of my breasts could be seen, and its back was practically nonexistent. A mirror, as I turned my head to stare at myself, showed just the top of my buttock cleavage. I opted for a gold body-chain to go about my slim waist.

I was ready, naked under the gown and with my bare feet inside the Kimel evening pumps, when Bocca Carducci opened the door. Donna had spent some time on my red hair, it was coiffed beautifully and set here and there with rhinestone clips that had been in the jewel box Joe Turessi provided for his call girls.

Donna said, "You're exquisite."

I smiled and curtseyed. His eyes fell to the opening of the evening gown and the breasts he could see nestled there. When I rose, he offered me his arm.

We met Francesco Galuppo in the downstairs hall.

Both he and Bocca were wearing Austin-Hill suits, with Oleg Cassini ties and silk shirts. I assumed they wanted to display their money, here on the Riviera. Well, the image of the Mafia mobsters had changed a bit over the past decade, I guessed. They no longer appeared as the slant-hatted trigger men they had been in the early days of the Capone era. They are far more sophisticated, now. At least the bosses are.

The black Mercedes-Benz gathered us into its upholstered interior and the chauffeur took us by way of some narrow little streets out beyond the town of Saint Tropez and toward the hills behind it, which formed part of the Massif des Maures. It was a clear, balmy night in early summer, the stars were spangled across the dark blue sky to form a breathtaking tapestry. I sat with my thighs squeezed together, feeling the lust move in my veins slowly, like sap in a tree trunk. There was moisture at my hairy crotch, and my nipples tingled.

Donna had done a good job on me, I thought. I wondered if her ministrations were to be wasted. I shivered, though the night was warm.

Light exploded against the night sky as we came to the crown of a hill and headed straight on the road. In the distance I could make out what seemed to be a forest of illuminated trees. Bulbs of many colors hung there, it was as if all the Christmas trees in the world had been gathered by magic into one spot on Earth and brilliantly lighted.

"My God," I breathed.

"The Countess is known for her extravagances," Francesco Galuppo said heavily, as though he disapproved. "She spares no expenses, none at all."

And Bocca leaned closer to me as he chuckled. "Francesco has a computer for a mind. He calculates the cost of all this and thinks of how many starving Italians he could feed with the money this costs."

"And this is nothing," nodded Frankie boy. "Wait, wait."

The road veered to the left where it continued on to Saint Maxime. To the right, just at the bend, stood twin towers of stone with a heavy iron gate set on gigantic iron hinges. There was a coat of arms on each gate but all I could see of it as the Mercedes-Benz flashed past was a lion rampant. Then we were moving up the gravel drive toward a gaggle of Lincoln Continentals, Rolls Royces, Cadillacs and a few scattered Porsches and Fiats.

The villa itself was a tremendous building, with all the electric lights inside it turned on, and quite a few outside. Those lights made daylight out of the grounds. There was a number of tiled roofs belonging to the villa, some at different levels than others, as though parts of the main building had been added with the years. The windows were tall, many-paned, and hung with curtains that hid everything but the light behind them. I could hear music as Francesco opened the door.

With the music came the sound of voices, of laughter, of here and there a shrill feminine voice protesting a liberty or an indiscretion. My eyes went to lawned terraces and marble statues, to a staircase of low, stone treads fanning outward toward a fountain and a large pool lit from underneath by a battery of floodlamps. Hedges and trees formed little mazes, here and there, where men and women walked and chatted.

"Come," said Bocca. "We must pay our respects."

We moved up marble steps toward a magnificent foyer, the stone walls of which were covered with magnificent tapestries. The ceiling was domed, there were vases of flowers everywhere, and where the tapestries did not cover them, the walls were hung with paintings.

The Countess was slim radiance in red taffeta. She was a handsome woman, somewhere in her early forties I guessed, with a thick mane of black hair piled high on her head and hung with strands of little pearls. A rope of pearls was at her throat, her fingers flashed with pearl rings set with diamonds. She exuded sex appeal, her firm breasts were like marble, half visible in the low decolletege.

She turned to our approach, held out her bare right arm. Intense black eyes went from Francesco to Bocca and settled on yours truly. Laughter was in those eyes, and a vast flirtatiousness.

"Francesco, my darling! And sweet, golden Bocca! How good of you to come. This makes everything worthwhile."

To my surprise, Frankie boy bowed from the waist while he kissed her extended hand as might any diplomat. "The pleasure and the honor is ours, dear Countess."

Bocca also kissed that hand, bowing deeply. Over his downbent head her black eyes ran over my body. The plucked eyebrows lifted.

"And this gorgeous beauty! *Qui est la?* Who is she?"

The introductions were made, I curtseyed gracefully, barely touching the warm fingers she gave my hand. Her fingers tightened on mine, drew me closer. The black eyes went to my companions.

"How long have you two had this magnificent creature hidden away in that house of yours? No, no. Never mind telling me. It is enough that you have finally decided to let her be seen. Now come with me, all of you. We must have our apertif."

The apertif was *blanc-cassis*, which is nothing more than a blob of raspberry syrup at the bottom of a glass of chilled white wine. It was delicious and, I told myself, a little something more. The raspberry syrup would disguise a smidgeon of Spanish Fly, very comfortably. Or maybe it was my own excited flesh. At any rate, my erogenous zones began clamoring a few seconds after the *blanc-cassis* slid down my throat, and I noticed that both Bocca and Francesco were beginning to pant a little heavily.

The Countess trilled soft laughter as she put her arm about me, giving me a squeeze. "Now go mingle with the guests, all of you. There will be entertainment later, which I'm positive you'll all enjoy."

As she nodded a farewell, her hand slid down my flank and caressed my ungirdled rear end just for a second. I turned my head and winked at her.

Then we were moving toward the front door and out into the brightly lighted night, making our way to the gardens, to the maze of trees and hedges and finally down to the pool. Everywhere we went were waiters in white jackets, quiet and almost unnoticeable, carrying trays of wineglasses filled to their brims.

Bocca and Francesco chose Riviera Negroni's—a blend of gin, red vermouth, Campari and triple sec —while I contented myself with another *blanc-cassis*. This one, so far as my taste buds could tell, contained no aphrodisiac.

I told myself I walked in a dream world. Sure, sure, I knew there were people who lived like this, who went to magnificent parties where money was no object, but this was a little too much. In one sense, this was like the condemned man's last meal, as far as where I was concerned. Certainly Bocca had lied when he'd told me he'd spoken to Joe Turessi on the phone. Which meant neither he nor Francesco trusted me. I was here on sufferance. At any moment, they would lower the boom.

My feet took me away from my two Mafia bosses, across a little stretch of lawn and to a marble bench placed before a stand of juniper trees. I sank down on the bench, began to assess my situation. I was here on my lonesome, though N.Y.M.P.H.O. knew about me—as witness that man in Orly Field air terminal who'd spoken to me—and there were a couple of Mafia men who had their doubts about me. I walked in the shadow of a cyanide bullet, no doubt about it.

It was incredible to me that a man like Frankie boy hadn't made that transatlantic phone call. Did he really believe me when I'd said that Turessi's phone had been tapped by U.S. narcotics agents? In that case, he might really send a man to the funeral home to check out Joe Turessi and report back to him. When he received that report, I was going to be one dead girl.

I was not happy. Still, I was alive.

And I could always say that Joe Turessi died after I left him. These mobsters couldn't prove any different, could they? Or—could they? I bit my lip and got even more unhappy.

My common sense told me to split this scene. It was getting more freaked out every second. I'd acted on impulse by coming here, I'd taken a big gamble because at the time it seemed the right thing to do. Now I wasn't so sure. But I'd already stuck my head in the lion's mouth.

And then I saw something that brought the fear into my throat, clawing, feeling vaguely like fish-hooks being dragged upward from my gut. A pair of yellow eyes was watching me! My heart slammed wildly even as I told myself to sit quietly, to pretend not to notice. Surely, there were no wild animals here in the Fouquet gardens!

I turned my head to stare toward the pool where shrieks of delight were shredding the night. But my eyes slid sideways, fastened on what was peeping from a stand of garrigue junipers.

Those were no animal eyes. Somebody was hidden in the trees, watching me through a pair of field glasses. The overhead yellow bulbs were reflected in its lenses, giving them that feral look.

Now who in hell was so interested in Cherry Delight?

Certainly not Bocca Carducci and Francesco Galuppo! All they had to do to watch my movements was accompany me wherever I went at the party. No, this was someone else. A member of my own organization? Could be, but I doubted it.

I got the feeling I was caught up in a whirlpool of plot and counterplot. The Mafia boys I could understand, but who else was there in this corner of the Riviera who wanted to watch what I did? It made no sense.

The last of the *blanc-cassis* went down my throat. I rose to my feet and walked away from the bench toward the pool where the shrieks and cries were getting wilder. Maybe the orgy was about to begin, but I had work to do.

I slipped close to a big yew hedge and ran along it. The man with the field glasses was on the other side of the hedge and I wanted to have a closer look at him. I ran until the hedge parted, then peered through. He was halfway across the lawn, walking toward a group of statues framing a small fountain.

There was no hiding place between him and me, so I crouched down, waiting. He moved toward the statues, turned and stared in my direction. I don't believe he could see me, I was behind the hedge and my evening gown was black; the pool with all the yelling men and women around it was behind me, maybe it was there that his stare went.

His searching look seemed to reassure him. He took something out of his pocket—by straining my eyes I made out a pair of field glasses—and put a hand to a marble cupid. The cupid moved, toppled to one side. The man slid the field binoculars into a space at the base of the statue, then let the cupid slide back into place.

Once more he turned, stared around him. He moved off at a rapid walk toward some trees. He did not look behind him, now.

I waited about ten minutes. Then I sauntered away from the hedge, toward the little fountain. I walked casually, as if admiring the lawn and the gardens. Not until I was near the marble cupid did I turn and let my eyes go in the direction where the man had walked. There was no one there.

My hand touched the cupid, pushed. With a faint creak of protesting iron hinges, the statue moved up and away from the hiding place inside its base. I reached in, brought out the field glasses. I turned them over and over, I could see nothing odd about them; they were merely high-powered binoculars. I put them to one side, reached into the hollow space and found it empty. I put the field glasses back, and let the statue topple into place.

I walked away from the fountain and the statues, puzzled. Obviously, that hollow marble base was some sort of dead drop, where messages or other things could be put so a fellow spy could pick them up when needed. But what was so unusual about a pair of binoculars? The more I thought about it, the curiouser I became, as Alice might have said of Wonderland.

When I came to the hedge I hid behind it and waited.

A different man was coming along the forest pathway toward the cupid. He pushed the statue aside, reached in and brought out the binoculars. He slipped them into his pocket and walked off. I stared after him, scowling.

What in hell was going on?

There had been no hidden camera in the glasses, I'd made sure of that. They were binoculars, nothing more, nothing less. Why be so secretive about them?

The two men who were so interested in those field glasses must have a purpose for their use. What was that purpose? Certainly not to spy on the carry-ings-on of the people at the party! All they had to do—just as I intended doing in a few seconds—was walk forward and join anybody at all.

I walked toward poolside while I concentrated about the men and the binoculars. Suddenly a man leaped at me, a big grin on his face as his arms wrapped around me. Off to one side, I caught a glimpse of a woman with her skirt up to her bare behind and her front plastered to that of a young man with curly black hair, swapping spit with his mouth. There was another man with his hands inside the low bodice of a woman's evening gown, fingers kneading her big white breasts.

The party was getting a hot on.

Everywhere I looked, even while the hands of the Frenchman who had me in his arms were sliding all over my bare back where there was no gown to cover it, men and women were shedding their inhibitions, along with their clothes. I saw one man on his knees between the stockinged legs of a girl whose skirt was up to her bellybutton, his hands clinging to her thighs while his lips browsed on her shaven private parts. Another man was standing with a woman, hands sunk into her pudding-soft behind while his hips lurched and drove his male shaft between the lips of her feminine *con*.

"How'd it get started so fast?" I asked rather dazedly.

The man with me chuckled thickly. "You didn't see the water ballet? My dear dolly, you missed the fireworks. But come! Some of it may still be going on."

He turned me with a hand inside my low gown-back, his palm and fingers lazily caressing my buttocks while they wobbled while I walked, bringing me with him to poolside. There were still some naked performers in the water, a couple of girls and boys locked with each other in the popular Venus reverse posture, hips gently moving as their arms and hands acted as paddles to keep them afloat. I saw teams of male and female, their bodies joined at their genitals, half lying on their backs as they floated, moving inside and out.

"They came down the steps stark naked," cackled my companion. "They began to play around on the edge of the pool, toying with each other. Then they dove into the pool and began doing what comes naturally."

His big middle finger was between my thighs, gently working around in my moist genital trench. He was in his middle years, partially bald, with a hooked nose and a fleshy mouth: not exactly an Adonis. But he was touched by Dionysius, by which I mean he was sloshed to the gills, and his tongue wagged as though on springs. I threw my arms about his neck and rubbed my breasts to his chest.

"Tell me more," I cooed.

"The Countess is known for her parties. I think she has outdone herself this time. Once in a while she'll have a boy and a girl up from the village to put on a sex show for her guests, but tonight—ah, it's as if she'd thrown financial discretion to the winds. And that's a strange thing, too. . . ."

"Why is that? Isn't she rich?"

He was nuzzling my throat with his lips, kissing my shoulders where the evening gown bared them. "Everybody thinks so. I know better. I'm a banker, dear. It's my business to know the financial status of my clients. And I number the Countess Colette de Vaux among those."

My head was whirling, and not from the fact that his fingers were rumpling up my gown so that more and more of my bare legs and upper thighs were coming into view. First, the men with the binoculars. Now this revelation about *la Comtesse*. If she didn't have the bread to give a party like this—who was supplying her with the money?

I asked the old goat about that, and he chuckled thickly. "Let's go somewhere private, my love. You are getting me very excited. I haven't been this hot in a long time."

My left thigh did the walking for me along his front and found something that vaguely resembled a long thin stick jutting up from his groin. Well, well! My boy friend wasn't as old as I thought. My hand slid down between us, moved up and down his erection. I felt him buck and jerk against me as he started panting like a spavined horse.

"You will tell me what I wish to know?" I whispered.

"About the Countess? Eh, why not?"

I let him turn me, lead me away from the pool and up the staircase. We passed a man crouched between the widespread knees of a woman, her stockinged legs uplifted, the myriad light from the pool gleaming on her pallid thighflesh as she squirmed and scrunched against him. I could hear the slurping sound of his male organ as it went in and out of her vaginal channel. To one side of them and up a few steps, a woman had opened her dress and lifted out a big, blue-veined breast which she was feeding to one of the naked young performers.

"Why?" I asked. "Why does the Countess give such parties? Yes, yes, they make her popular. I can understand that. But. . . ."

His chuckle was lewd. "She makes friends, hein? And friends tell her things she wants to know."

Understanding hit me like a sledgehammer. Me, idiot! I should have doped this out myself. "Blackmail," I whispered.

His shoulders made an elaborate shrug. "It is how I have figured it out, dolly. She learns things about you, about me—have you a husband you don't want to know about this night, *cherie?*—and files them away somewhere against the need for francs. It must be that way, it can be no other."

We ran side by side into the villa. My dirty older man had me ready for fun and games with a vengeance. My blood was pounding, I couldn't think straight. His fingers were like electric wires running over my hips inside my evening gown, they slid over my quivering buttocks and then around to my front to tousle my pubic hairs and hunt for my erect clitoral bud. He knew his way around a woman, did this lecher.

The cantharides that had been in the first *blanc-cassis* I'd had didn't hurt, either. And the going-over by Donna was an added bit of erotica that was firing my nerve-ends.

I dragged my companion into a nearby room. I wondered where Bocca Carducci and Francesco Galuppo might be right about now, but the hell with the Mafia mobsters at a time like this. I had been working steadily for my organization ever since I'd gone into that coffin, so right now I was going to do something nice for Cherry Delight.

I pushed my companion into a straightbacked chair, panting. "We'll try the *dok el arz* posture."

He grinned up at me, watching me lift the black satin skirt of my gown. "Ah, you know the Sheik Nefzawi and his writings?"

My lips gave him a wicked smile. "Honey, I've studied the old masters until my eyes popped out. Nefzawi, Ovid, Aloysia, Sigea, Philaenis and Elephantine, you name 'em, I've read 'em. You might call it a hobby of mine. Or an avocation. I have a good body, I enjoy sexual acrobatics from time to time if not all the time, and what I enjoy I try to make as perfect as possible."

"An excellent credo, indeed," he nodded.

I stood between his legs, pushing down the straps of the gown. I eased the bodice to my middle and gave my shoulders a little shimmy. My breasts danced up and down for his bulging eyes. My brown nipples were long and thick, my breastflesh was smooth and solid.

"Like a milk shake, honey?" I giggled.

I shook my love jugs for him, head back and my red hair starting to come loose from the pins and pearl-strands holding it. His whimpers and groans of enjoyment were music to my ears. Then I pushed the rest of the gown off and stood naked between his legs, wearing only my rhinestoned Kimels.

I bent, breasts dangling, and put my hands to his zipper.

In another moment he was out there in the open, long and thin, quivering in his excitement. My fingertips went up and down his erection, lazily. My backbone bent a little more so I could brush his swollen penishead with my bloated nipples. He whinnied like a stallion enjoying a cute little mare.

"You know, I don't even know your name," I breathed.

"*Ma poupee cherie!* At a time like this, you ask for names! Eh, *bien*. I am Etienne Montaigne. Now that that's settled. . . ."

"I'm Cherry Delight. And since my name is Cherry, I like to ride a cock horse."

He whinnied laughter, sobbing and panting in his desire for the body I was showing him, standing between his thighs. I lifted my left leg casually, telling him to put his knees together. He gave my wet labia a good long look before he did what I told him, so that I found myself straddling his trousered legs.

Then I sat down on him, slowly. He went in with a lazy lasciviousness that added to our mutual pleasure. I rested my behind on his shaking legs and—as I'd done with Joe Turessi—let my constrictor muscles ripple up and down. Etienne Montaigne sobbed as he shook to that cunnectasiac caress.

I set out to make a friend of this older Frenchman. He was a banker, he might even lend me money if I needed it. Remember now, I was on my own here on the Riviera, I wasn't about to overlook any bets when it came to feathering my nest. You never know, in my line of work, where you'll have to turn in an emergency. So I let myself post up and down on his rigid manhood, giving him a couple of additional thrills by leaning forward and letting him have my nipples for his pouting lips, one after the other.

I am an adept when it comes to sex. I've made a thorough study of the subject, going back to the days when I'd immersed myself in my father the doctor's medical texts. At one time I'd even thought of studying medicine myself, but then I met Mark Condon and he talked me into becoming a member of the Mafia-fighting set.

My study of medicine and its corresponding knowledge of the human body stood me in good stead as a N.Y.M.P.H.O. girl, however. Like now, for instance, giving old Etienne Montaigne his Jack Straw jollies. My right hand went down beneath his scrotum and my fingernails played at spider's legs with his testicles, in a little rogering refinement that heaped some extra thrills on his male love-nerves.

But I didn't hurry him. Oh, my. No! There is a way to help the male last and last, if his female companion in the amorous arts is willing to play her proper part. When his penis swelled, I tightened my constrictor cunnae muscles on it, just holding it, while I ceased all movement of my thighs and hips. As the crisis passed, I let those interior muscles loosen, tighten, loosen, as I began once more to go up on and down on him.

"Ma colombe! Mon ange!" he sobbed, his body shaking all over in the delirious delights flooding it. "Mmmmmm, *ca ira! Je me sens mal. . . ."*

He whispered and moaned, babbled and blurted out love words in French that I followed well enough to know I was making the most fantastic impression on him. At that moment I could have had anything I wanted of the old guy. And he would be looking forward to a repeat performance by yours truly. You can't have me just once, to para-phrase a teevee commerical, once only whets the appetite. He would need some more of my puden-dal pleasures when he recovered from this bout.

Which was as it should be. I needed friends on the Riviera.

But all good things have to come to an end. So I made it a most pleasant ending for Etienne Mon-taigne, doing a bump and grind and using those in-side muscles of mine until he was jellying and shud-dering and contorting under me until I began to think he was taking leave of his senses. His eyes opened once as he stared up at me in utter adora-tion. I was Venus and Astarte, Inninuinni and Isis to him, all the love goddesses of history rolled up in one.

"Tu es la plus belle fille du monde!" he breathed.

That was when he fainted.

I climbed off him after a few moments. He was still alive, he hadn't pulled a Joe Turessi on me. I figured all he needed was a little catnap. I rear-ranged his clothing, then slithered back into my Givenchy evening gown. While he slumbered on, I thought maybe I could find out a little more about this villa Fouquet.

My feet carried me from the tiny reading room we'd made our own, out into the hall. The party was still going on, but by this time, a younger crowd had taken over, probably because the younger ones had more sexual stamina. There were naked couples banging each other in the shadows, on the big marble staircase, even using the chairs pushed back against the wall.

I skirted them, evading a hand here and a hand there that sought to drag me down and make a *seance a trois* out of what was now a *seance a deux*. I laughed and blew kisses and wandered up the staircase and along a carpeted hall between rows of oil paintings, past open doors through which I could see groups of men and women grappling together in various erotic entanglements.

I was sorely tempted to join a few of these groupings. There was one set of naked bodies where three men were enjoying one woman who was having a ball but who was obviously outnumbered. I watched them. One man lay on his back with the woman on top of him, a second man knelt behind her with his male tool thrust deep into her behind, while a third crouched before her face and working mouth. She needed help, but her happy groans told me she wasn't asking for any.

I moved on, feeling my blood churning hotly.

I didn't find out where Francesco Galuppo was hiding himself, but I did discover Bocca Carducci. He and a blonde doll were silently writhing on top of a bed. Bocca was between her wideflung thighs, sawing in and out of her moist femininity with an outsized organ. I could hear his grunts and her bleats from the doorway.

My eyes took in her nakedness in a girdle and black nylon stockings. Her big breasts were outside a brassiere, held up by its rolled cups, while she had unfastened the garterclasps of the girdle so her stockings wouldn't ladder. She was a meaty dish, not fat but with plenty of good flesh on her bones. Her breasts were bouncing and her thighs were shimmying as she lurched and stabbed herself on the rigid shaft impaling her.

From their bodies, my eyes went to the window.

I froze, standing motionless.

Those feral yellow eyes were out there in a tree, peering avidly in at the blonde Italian and his bed partner! I could hardly believe what I was seeing. If that voyeur had wanted, he could have walked right into the room and stood beside me, for all Bocca and the woman would care. They were deep in their carnal coupling, oblivious to the rest of the world.

I had to warn Bocca about those field glasses. Maybe he would know more about the men using them than I. I didn't want to yell the alarm, I wasn't sure how the blonde who was banging her rump up and down on the bedcoverings would react. I had to be a little subtle about it.

Well, hell. I was a woman with the hots, right? What could be more natural than for me to want a little of what Bocca was giving the blonde?

I ran up into the room, bent to grasp the hem of

the Givenchy gown. Out of the corner of my eyes, I saw a faint movement of the binoculars. Nosey-guts had seen me come in. I'd show him something else.

The gown came up, my nudity came into view. I tossed the evening gown through the air. Then I hipswung over to the side of the bed. I stood there a few seconds, using my hands to lift and shake my breasts, to caress them, to pull the big brown nipples out and twirl them between my forefingers and thumbs.

It would seem perfectly obvious to the man with the binoculars that I was a woman with the hots, I was seeing another woman getting what I wanted from Bocca Carducci. I was playing with myself, working my *con* into a lather so I could join the couple on the bed and practice a little troilism with them.

I put a knee on the bed and a hand on Bocca's bare back. He jerked at my touch and turned a surprised face toward me. I put my face toward his as though to kiss him.

But before our lips could meet, I breathed, "There's a man with a pair of binoculars in a tree just outside the window of this room. Do you know anything about him?"

Poor Bocca couldn't think straight. His glazed blue eyes told me he was in the throes of an oncoming orgasm. But my hand was dipping between his thighs, to grip his testicles. To prevent that orgasm, I gave his balls a hard squeeze.

Trust Cherry Delight to lend a guy a helping hand.

Chapter Four

Bocca Carducci turned an agonied face toward me.

I gave him a happy grin and took away my hand, letting the fingernails play at spiders' legs along his testicles to make up for the pain I'd caused him. Beneath him the blonde woman opened her eyes, stared up at me disbelievingly.

"How about letting me in on the game?" I breathed.

"Qui es la?" asked the blonde woman.

"A friend of mine," grunted Bocca. "What's the idea, Cherry?"

I lifted a bare leg and put it over the blonde lady so she had a terrific view of my private parts. Then I lowered myself right onto her face and tightened my inner thighs around her ears so she couldn't hear a thing.

Her hands slid up over my thighs to my behind.

Before she could push me off, I whispered to Bocca, "There's a man out there in a tree with a pair of binoculars who's looking in on us."

His head turned, his eyes went to the window. From that angle, he couldn't see the man. He growled, "You sure? I don't like to make love in public."

I told him about the man who'd been watching me down in the gardens. "Why, Bocca? Why should anyone be so interested in me? Or in you either, for that matter?"

He grinned, his eyes on my hanging breasts as I crouched over his lady fair. "So you're a good looking girl, he likes to look at pretty women. And—" his shoulders shrugged in a typically Latin gesture, "he likes to watch a real man in action."

The hands in my buttock flesh had not pushed me off, as I'd expected. Instead, fingers were tightening in my gluteus maximus, were holding me to the mouth that was feasting on my *con*. I quivered as I felt a tongue titillate my rigid clitoris, grew excitedly aware of that tongue sliding back and forth on my labia. My hips jerked in a reflex motion.

Whether I wanted it or not, the Frenchwoman was drawing me into their vortex of pleasure. My senses swam, my eyes lidded and my mouth came open to aid my breathing. And then Bocca had to lower his head and nuzzle at my breast, to draw my bloated brown nipple between his lips.

His loins picked up the speed of his ramming, I could hear a slurping sound as his hard flesh went into and retreated from her wet flesh. She moaned—I could feel it in that private part of me— and her hips jounced and bounced.

They went at it hammer and tongs.

She went at me lips and tongue.

I yelled, I couldn't help it. My excitement was too wild to keep smothered inside me. Pretty soon Bocca was grunting and groaning, his body shaking. The Frenchwoman was making sounds, too, but my *con* was smothering them.

Bocce slowed the movement of his hips. He wasn't spent, not yet, he was getting his second wind. He rested a moment, his blue eyes burning into mine. I raised up a little, heard the blonde sobbing air into her tortured lungs. I waited in the frog position, my pulses pounding, my nooky nerve-ends quivering.

There was more to come, I knew it.

Bocce was hardening again inside the woman. His faint grin told me that, as well as the slow pumping of his loins. The blonde moaned. I felt her tonguetip stab up at me. That tongue slid around and around, lazily. Then as her lover started to move faster, her tongue dipped and darted with increasing speed.

I told myself to forget the man in the tree. Hell! I had forgotten him.

Who could think at a time like this, when sensation was alive in my body, when soft lips suckled my nipples, one after the other, and a hard little tongue reamed at will where I was every inch a female? My hips picked up their beat, my buttocks looped and swung, and pretty soon I was resting on her open mouth and giving it all I had.

All good things must come to an end. We finished at about the same time, sobbing and grunting, panting and cursing. We clung to each other in the final throes of diddling dissolution.

I rolled off and lay on my back, staring blindly up at the ceiling. I may be a Mafia sexterminator, but right now my body was just being me. Cherry Delight, in the pleasant throes of an amoral aftermath. A soft hand slid along my bare thigh, up to my red pubic bush, and fingernails tickled.

"That was wonderful," a soft voice announced. "I 'ave not 'ad such fun in a long, long time. *C'est si on faisait ca d'une autre maniere?*"

I raised up on an elbow. "Try it another way? Aren't you tired?"

Her soft laughter rang out. "Cherie, I could go on and on. I can nevaire get enough of loving."

She sounded like a girl after my own heart. I'm not exactly a nympho, but when goodies are offered, a gal has to be crazy to turn them down. My eyes went to Bocca Carducci.

"How about it, Bocca?" I asked. "Another go?"

"Wait," he said.

He rose from the bed and turned to face the window. He had a terrific body, lean and hard, with muscles bulging out all over him. His foremost muscle was not quite limp, it showed itself proudly, but there was a scowl on his face.

Bocca let me see the scowl. "You are sure?" His head jerked toward the window. I nodded. Almost regretfully, he sighed, smiled down at the blonde woman.

"I'm sorry, Aimee. Something's just come up."

"So I see," she smiled lewdly, eyes fastened on his pushy priapus.

He really was getting bigger, eyeing us two luscious lovebombs naked on the bed. Aimee lay with her stockinged legs sprawled apart, letting him see the moistness of her nooky need, while I wasn't in a much more modest pose, myself.

Still, he shook his head. "No go, girls. I have work to do."

He reached for his shorts that lay across a chairback. I sighed and got to my knees, knowing that Aimee was smiling invitingly at me, that her gaze was zeroing in on my mons veneris.

"Another time," I said with a shrug of smooth shoulders that set my breasts in motion.

All I had to do was lift my evening gown and let it drop around my nudity. Bocca Carducci took a little longer, but he was dressed soon enough, and went to the edge of the bed and kissed Aimee on her lips, her nipples and for a brief moment, on the honey-pot between her thighs.

His hand caught my elbow, turned me toward the door. As we went along the hall, he asked more questions about the man, so I told him about the statue that slid back and the binoculars that were nothing but binoculars.

He eyed me curiously. "You're pretty smart for a dame to think of something like that. Examining those binoculars, I mean."

"Joe baby taught me all the tricks," I smiled happily. "In Uncle Sam country, a lot of different law people take an interest in the Family. They use all kinds of tricks, so a girl has to be on her toes. At first I thought those field glasses were fitted with some sort of air gun that could fire a poisoned pellet. You know? But there wasn't anything like that."

He nodded; said, "We got to find Francesco."

Francesco Galuppo could be anywhere, but we finally discovered him lying flat on his back on the grass outside, arms flung wide, his eyes closed. Oh, no, he wasn't dead. Far from it. He was as big as life, standing up proudly at his hairy groin, with a pair of very white breasts wrapped around his manshaft and with a pair of soft red lips sliding up and down on it.

The woman who was orally operating on him was in her early thirties, with black hair tumbling about her face and bare shoulders. Her dress was pulled down to her bellybutton and her big breasts slid around Frankie's organ while her head bobbed like a cork in rough water. Her skirt was up to her girdled behind, showing handsome legs in black nylons and very white, pallid thighs.

"Give him a chance," said Bocca hoarsely.

He was starting to breathe like a spavined horse again, and I could feel my own tail temperature rising. His hands were on my hips, one palm pushed me. He wanted me to bend over before him and spread my legs.

Why not? He had a goodie for me, and I sure could use what he had. My hands raised my skirt, I bent as he said and felt him crowding up behind me. He went in slowly, slowly, while we both watched Frankie boy and the nearly naked woman.

There are fringe benefits to my job. This was one of them. I panted and pushed back at him, and when he was fully seated, I swung my hips in that special way of mine that increases the pleasure of a man. I bucked and bumped, and Bocca sobbed and twisted behind me.

Finally Francesco Galuppo could stand no more. His hands lifted from the grass, caught the woman's head and held her firmly while he arched upward from the lawn and did some bone bucking himself. Bocca and I stared, our erotic excitement increased by what we were seeing.

Finally I tightened up on Bocca Carducci and let

my constrictor muscles go to work. He damned near collapsed on top of me before he was done. I supported his weight, let him pull himself together and out of me. Then I straightened and shook my skirt down around my legs.

Frankie saw us just about then.

Worry tightened his dark features. "What's up?"

"Nothing—right now," I grinned.

Bocca growled, "Come on. We got to blow. Tell you in the car."

The blackhaired woman protested, sitting up, "Hey, what about me?"

"You'll find somebody, honey," Frankie told her, patting her head. "And thanks. You were great, simply great."

She stared at us almost with tears in her eyes. I felt sorry for her. She'd gone all out to please Francesco Galuppo and now he was leaving her high—though not very dry, I'd bet.

I ran over, said, "If you dig the lez, there's a blonde woman upstairs on a bed, all nice and bare, just waiting. . . ."

She smiled faintly, nodded.

Then I was running after my two Mafia bosses. Bocca was filling Frankie in on the details when I joined them. Francesco stared at me coldly, as though I might be to blame for this. He had been called away from his hot mamma, and wasn't too happy about it. Frankly, I didn't blame him.

"Well, it's true enough," I said defiantly.

"Bocca didn't see anybody in a tree."

"I did. And in the hedges, too."

He snorted, but he made no further effort to break free of our company and go back to his abandoned girl friend. We got into the Mercedes-Benz, woke up the chauffeur, and Frankie told him to take us home.

We rode through the Riviera night, beneath stars that were slowly paling before the coming dawn. It was not dawn yet, but there was a hint of coming sunlight on the horizon. We went along narrow little lanes and past darkened cottages and farmhouses, then came down the hill into Saint Tropez.

As the chauffeur braked before the house, Bocca reached into a special compartment of the tonneau, lifting out two Walthian Beretta automatics. He handed one to Francesco Galuppo who checked the magazine and snapped it shut.

"Just in case," Bocca said.

I noticed he kept his gun in his hand as he followed Frankie to the front door. Frankie unlocked the door, pushed it open cautiously. The interior was as dark as the inside of a whale's belly. And there was no sound.

"I don't like it," said Bocca, pushing past Frankie with his Beretta up.

"What's to like?" I wondered. "Everybody's asleep."

"Not Pietro. He waits in the downstairs hall for—"

Bocca swore. There was a dull sound and the explosion of a Walthian Beretta in the front hallway. Frankie screamed. "What is it? *Cosa e?*"

Bocca swore vividly. "Somebody—something—on the floor."

I sprang for the wall switch. The lights went on. One of the beefy men who'd met me at the Nice airport lay sprawled on the floor. Bocca was practically alongside him, having tripped over his body.

My knees were on the floor before either of them could move, my hand going to his chest. His heart was thumping at a pretty good rate.

"He's alive. He probably got knocked out."

Frankie helped me turn him. There was a lump the size of a punchball on the back of his head. "Cold water," I snapped. "Fill a pitcher."

Bocca nodded, got to his feet and ran.

When he came back with the pitcher, I poured it slowly over Petey's face. He didn't need the whole pitcher, he blinked when it was only half empty.

"Stop drownin' me," he gasped.

"What happened?" asked Frankie.

Pietro scowled, trying to remember. At last he shook his head. "I dunno, boss. I was sittin' here in the hall like I always do, when I heard a sound. I got up and the ceilin' fell in on me."

Bocca snarled some naughty Italian words under his breath, made a run for the living room. Lights flashed on. There were more naughty words in Italian. He came back into the hallway, stared at Frankie.

"Cherry was right. Those guys who were looking at us with field glasses were doing it for a reason—to make sure we were still at the party. The place has been turned upside down."

Frankie went white. He snarled and crouched, an animal hate gleaming in his eyes. The Beretta made a dark weight in his hand.

"They're long gone, Frankie," I told him.

"How do you know?" he snapped.

"Oh, come on. If they were watching us at the party, don't you think one of those boys would call the house and let whoever was here know when we were leaving?"

"She's right," said Bocca.

Francesco Galuppo straightened up, nodding. *"Si, si.* I didn't think for a minute. What did they—?" He broke off and stared hard at Bocca. The blonde man glanced at me and shrugged his shoulders. They must have thought I was a dummy. I could have told them both what the thieves were after. They wanted that gadget I was to take back to Joe Turessi. Any nincompoop could have guessed that.

I paid no attention to either of them. I started to help Pietro to his feet. He was still groggy, his hand went to that big lump on the back of his noggin, and when his fingers touched it, he winced.

"Into bed, Petey," I told him.

Frankie said, "She's right, Pietro. You need a good sleep. I'll get a doctor in the morning."

"Why do you need a doctor? If you have an ice-bag or ice water and some gauze, I'll make a compress for him. At least, it'll ease the tenderness. And you can have his skull x-rayed tomorrow, to make sure there's no concussion."

Frankie nodded. "Fine, fine. Bocca and I will get him to his room, there's an icebag in the medicine chest. And ice in the refrigerator."

In half an hour, I had Petey comfortable with an icebag on his head to reduce the swelling. By this time, Frankie and Bocca had made an investigation of the house and found it thoroughly ransacked.

Donna was tied up and unconscious in her room. They sent me to her, looking very grim, very up-tight about the whole thing.

I revived Donna with a little smelling salts. She was scared and I didn't blame her. "I don't know what happened," she told me tearfully. "I was asleep, as you can see. . . ."

She had on a baby doll nightie, sheer enough to see through and what there was to see was plenty. Her heavy breasts were pale, their nipples big and clearly visible through the pink nylon.

". . . and they must have come in then, with chloroform or something. I woke up, there was a soft pad at my nose, and I blanked out. What did they want?"

I shrugged, telling myself if Donna didn't know, it wasn't up to me to clue her in. She hugged herself, lying on the bed in an almost fetal position. She was still frightened.

"Where was the other one? The muscleman who came to get me at the airport?" I asked. "They got to Petey in the front hall."

"Tony? I don't know. Maybe he had the night off."

I patted her shoulder. "It doesn't make any difference. You go to sleep. Nothing will happen now."

I went downstairs where Francesco Galuppo and Bocca Carducci were seated in big wingchairs, staring at each other. The *capos* didn't like this caper, it didn't sit at all well with them. They looked a touch terrified, themselves, and I felt I knew the reason why.

"At least, they didn't get what they were after," I said cheerfully.

Frankie glowered at me. "How do you know that?"

Francesco was not a bright boy. He must have gotten to the rank of *capo* on his muscles alone. I said, "Because they were after the gadget, right? And if the gadget wasn't here to give to me, how could they have gotten it?"

He came up out of his chair as if I'd insulted him. "How can you know that? Who told you?"

"Nobody had to tell me. I can think."

He glowered at me. "You're too damn smart for your own good."

I shoved the needle in a little deeper. "Joe Turessi likes smart people around him. We have to be on our toes in our country."

He reached for me with a hamlike hand, all hairy on its back. I said, "Don't play rough, Frankie. I'm not Donna. I can't protect myself."

His surprise was ludicrous. Italian males like their females soft and obedient. They take a dim view of them when they make waves.

Bocca was grinning at us both. "Sit down, Frankie. Something tells me the lady means what she says. Although it would be interesting to see you two go at it."

Frankie snarled, "She insulted me. She as good as told me I'm dumb. If she's so smart, let her decide who goes to report to the boss of bosses about what happened here."

I waved a manicured hand. "No problem. You both go. That way, neither of you can rat on the other and if there's any blame, it falls on you both, not just on one."

"And leave you here alone?" he sneered.

I made my eyes get big. "Now even you can't think I'm the one who ransacked this house! Not even you, Frankie."

He was silent, but his dark eyes glared hate. I

think Francesco Galuppo half suspected that I'd had a hand in what had taken place here, even if I hadn't been on the premises. A tiny thought came into my mind: who had done the looting, and—why? Sure, sure. To get the gadget. But why did anybody want the thing? And—who wanted it?

I let my think tank work while I smiled at the glowering Frankie. Every once in a while, these Mafia families work themselves up into a feud. Somebody in the organization wants what somebody else has, there's a schism and a battle royal. At least, that's what happens in the United States. So why should France or Italy be an exception? The name of this particular game is vendetta.

"All I'll do while you're gone is show off my shape in a bikini and maybe get a nice suntan," I said lazily. "Oh, I'll hold the fort for you. I'll make sure nobody comes around looking for anything. I'll have Petey and Tony on twenty-four hour guard."

I sat up straight. "This time, nobody'll come crashing in to make a shambles of the house."

Bocca chuckled. "I believe she will, too."

Frankie grumbled. "I don't trust her."

I gave him the benefit of my teeth in a grin. "As for that, what makes you think I trust you, Frankie boy? I thought you had a nice, solid organization on this side of the Atlantic. First night I'm here, you damn near get robbed." I made a rude sound with my lips. "Some tight security, I must say. I'm just glad I work for Joe Turessi and not for you.

"Capo? You? Say rather, *capocchio!"*

He came for me then, his gorilla-like arms out to grab. I lifted a shoe and planted it in the middle of his hard belly. At the same time I grabbed one of those arms and yanked as my foot lifted.

So fast had been his rush that he furnished the momentum that lifted him upward and over my head. He flew through the air and came down on a little table, smashing the table and vase of flowers that had been standing on it. The sound of his landing shook the house.

I was on my feet, turning toward him in case he wanted to go on. He lay there dazedly, shaking his head. I told myself I had maybe made an enemy for sure, now. But I was tired of his goddamn suspicions, his hate-filled eyes and sneering mouth.

"Jeez," Bocca whispered, coming to stand beside me.

"He asked for it," I snapped.

"But—*capocchio?* That means 'silly', you know."

"He is silly. He's stupid. Why aren't you running this show, Bocca? You have looks, brains. Frankie boy thinks with his muscles. And badly."

The blue eyes studied me speculatively. They weighed me, judged me. After a moment he shook his head. "I can't quite figure you out. You're smart, damned sexy. What's a dame like you doing in the organization?"

"Joe pays me pretty good. Besides, I get extras. Like with you and Aimee tonight."

He grinned faintly. Right at that moment, Francesco Galuppo groaned. I ran around, lifted his head and put it on my thigh, kneeling beside him. When his eyes finally opened, they saw me beaming sympathetically down at him.

To my surprise, the hate was gone.

"You're tough tit, lady," he muttered. Respect gleamed in his black eyes as he asked, "You one of them women's lib girls we hear about?"

"I'm strictly family," I smiled. "And since I am, Frankie, how about shaking hands and saying no hard feelings?"

He held up his pawlike hand and shook mine. Seeing how Bocca was watching, Francesco growled, "She took me by surprise, Bocca. You hear?"

"I hear, Frankie."

"It couldn't happen again," I said sweetly, restoring to him some of his male pride.

"Damn right," he nodded, getting to his feet. He towered over me, he was a big one, but there was a grudging admiration on his face. "I like you, Cherry. I didn't before, I thought you were just a dumb dame. You're more than that."

"Now please, can I go to bed?" I asked.

Frankie grinned, clapped me on the back. "Go on, Cherry. You earned it. And you know, it might not be a bad idea for Bocca and me to go see the boss of bosses together." He guffawed. "I'd hate to see what's left of the guy who tried to bust into the house when you're here."

I blew them kisses and went off to beddy-bye.

I slept like the legendary log.

When morning came—late morning, it was past eleven as the bedside table clock told me—Donna was in the room, smiling cheerily, pulling back the curtains to let the Riviera sunlight into the room.

"You over the freak-out?" I asked.

She puzzled over the slang bit, but finally interpreted it correctly, nodding. "Oh, yes. I had a long sleep before you came to see me, and afterward. I'm fine, now."

"If the cook is in the kitchen, I'll have scrambled eggs and ham and a big pot of black coffee. Oh, yes. Orange juice, too. I'm in need of my vitamins."

Her eyes twinkled. "You had a big night." She tiptoed close to the bed to whisper, "Did you really do that to Francesco? Throw him over a chair, I mean?"

"It was luck," I eyed her a moment, asked, "How'd you find out?"

"Bocca told me."

I threw back the bedclothes and sheathed my body in a black Riviera bikini, which is about the scantiest bikini of them all, and then slid into a black knitted jump suit. The mirror showed a lot of my skin through the holes in the jump suit, which clung to me like wet silk, so I figured I was dressed just about right for walking on the promenade from the Hotel de la Tour to the Boutique Vachon.

Bocca Carducci and Francesco Galuppo were finished with their breakfasts when I came downstairs to join them, they were sipping coffee and looking thoughtful. Their eyes bulged a little when I walked into the room, which I took as a compliment to my girlish contours, and Bocca even smiled.

"We're going to fly to Sicily today," he told me. "We think it's a good idea, leaving you here to watch over things."

"You can take care of yourself," growled Frankie with a grumpy sound in his throat that was meant to be a chuckle.

"How long will you be gone?"

Bocca shrugged. "Two days, maybe three. Depends on what the don has to say. We'll tell him about you, he'll like what he hears. He may have great things in mind for you, Cherry."

I saw them off at the front door, then grabbed up my fringed shoulder bag and set out on foot for the promenade. I strolled along that five hundred yard long walkway, gathering stares and admiring whistles as cheese draws mice. I let my loosely confined breasts shake and jiggle, I made my buttocks twitch. I wanted to let people see me, to know I was alive.

An idea was burrowing around in my head, after the events of last night. Obviously, somebody besides the regular Mafia wanted that gadget. But who?

The answer had to be, another branch of the Family. Now feuds and fights are nothing common in the Brotherhood. There was the Castellammarese War, some years back in Uncle Sam land, and every once in a while somebody gets a contract for the hit on a *capo* who's offended the Mob, which often starts off another feud.

If two branches of the Fratellanza were sparring to get in a knockout blow here on the Riviera—as well as laying hands on that gadget—I wanted to know about it. Of course, somebody else might be horning in on the action, but I didn't go for that, it was the Mob that had killed some scientist to lay hands on his invention, and your Sicilian gangster is very close-mouthed indeed when it comes to blabbing to strangers.

Some of them have been hung on meathooks for less.

So I let myself be seen, in more ways than one. Everybody who'd been at that villa party had seen me there with Bocca and Frankie if they were at all interested in the Mafia. So word might get back to the other side that I was wandering around alone.

I left the promenade after a while and headed my feet for the Epi-plage beach. Now the Epi-plage has not the finer sands of the Tahiti or the Bouillabaisse beaches, but for some reason it is more fashionable.

There were boys and girls, men and women sprawled or sitting in various stages of nudity on beach blankets or beach chairs when I made my appearance. I slithered out of the jump suit, making a real production of it so every male eye would take in the lush shapes of my breasts, scarcely hidden by what served as a Bikini swimsuit bra. I bent over to slide it down my body, making sure my buttocks—naked except for two spaghetti straps that held the black vee across my mons veneris—were visible to all.

I stretched, I yawned a little, then walked toward the water. Everyone was watching me. I had shaken out my long red hair so it fell halfway down my back, and let my hips twitch to my every stride.

I swam out a good distance, then floated.

Somebody on a sleek white yacht hallooed and waved. I waved back, but I paid him no further mind. Folks are friendly in St. Tropez, for the most part.

I was halfway in to shore when a motor caught my ears and then a Chrysler Courier 229 that served as yacht's tender moved into my sight. I stopped swimming, paddled as the boat stopped its twin engines and drifted. A man leaned across the moldboard and nodded at me.

"Bonjour, ma'mselle," called Etinne Montaigne.

My old goat friend of the night before was dressed in a loose shirt and drill pants, with a yachting cap tilted on his head. He called, "Come aboard the Alsace. The Countess wants you to have a drink with her."

"I'll be delighted," I said.

He helped me into the tender. I sank my naked behind on a sun-heated cushion, and let his eyes crawl all over me on the way to the big white yacht.

"Don't you have a job to go to, Etienne?" I wondered.

He whinnied laughter. *"Ma belle*, this is my job, enjoying life. I have reached the age when I have made my millions. I have a good staff of workers at my banks. *Voila!* There is little for me to do, *hein?* So I enjoy myself."

"You have it made," I smiled.

I gave him an added thrill by going up the boat ladder ahead of him. He had a perfect view of my long, sleek legs, my moving buttocks and what lay in between my soft upper thighs, scarcely hidden by the bikini bottom. He was panting, and not from the exertion of the climb, when I stepped out onto the deck.

The *Alsace* was a sixty footer, a gorgeously trim, polished cabin cruiser that could cruise at twenty-two knots, Etienne told me as we padded across the gleaming deck with its brass trimmings. At one time it had belonged to a Greek shipping magnate who'd built himself a bigger sea palace at his own ship-yards. Etienne had been able to pick it up for a song.

The Countess came to meet us, her all but naked body in a plain bikini with about as much cloth to it as my own. And since she was built on a more majestic scale, her overlarge breasts shook so ripely I was afraid they were going to fall out of the tiny cups that barely covered her big brown nipples. Those mountainous mammaries shook more than somewhat even as her full thighs did a mild shimmy.

"Darling," she breathed. "It's so good to see you again."

She came right up to me, pressing her nakedness to mine. She was an attractive woman, with a lot of bare flesh. Her arm slipped around my middle and hugged me. So I hugged her.

"Etienne told me he had a marvelous time with you last night," she enthused, her dark eyes glittering strangely behind the long false black eyelashes. When she gestured, the Riviera sunshine caught the diamonds in her rings and made them sparkle.

I cast an arch glance at the simpering banker. "Etienne is a naughty boy to tell tales out of school."

"Ma columbe, don't mind us. We live in this world just for pleasure. You know? We have too much money and nothing to spend it on but our own whims and desires."

We came to a table covered with snowy cloth and two glasses filled with liquor, and a half full ashtray. The Countess gestured me into a wicker chair between hers and the one Etienne sank into with a sigh.

I ordered a *un dry*, which is what the French call a martini, then sat back to let my eyes assess the gleaming blue waters, the graceful luxury of the *Alsace*, and finally my companions.

The Countess sipped a *cassis*, as did Etienne.

"We are having a bash tonight on shipboard, darling," she said softly, her dark eyes caressing my exposed flesh. "We want you to come."

"I'll be delighted," I exclaimed. "I'm a bit lonesome, all by myself in that big house. Bocca and Frankie have gone off somewhere—they didn't say where or why—and I'm at wit's end for amusement."

"Oh, perfect," smiled Colette de Vaux. "And don't dress, it's just a casual thing." I might have been mistaken, but it seemed to me the she exchanged a meaning glance with my old goat friend.

"The less, the better," whinnied Etienne Montaigne, "because there won't be so much to take off."

"Nude swimming, of course," murmured the Countess.

We chatted about the film festival at Cannes and the entries for this year's competition. We discussed the merits of Bonnard and Braque as painters, the flavor of *rouille* as served with fish soup. Light, gay, inane talk, nothing serious. It was almost as if the *comtesse* and her banker friend were out to impress me with the insipidity of their lives.

I stayed on to sample a *salade nicoise*, made up of eggs, radishes, tomatoes, anchovies and peppers, onions and olives bedded down on chicory and lettuce.

Etienne carried me back to the beach in the tender in the middle of the afternoon. He told me to take a nap, to rest for the evening, and not to eat. There would be a feast on board the *Alsace*, and my belly must be empty to savor properly all the many goodies.

I slid into my jumpsuit, headed homeward.

Since I'd already planted the idea in the Countess' head that Bocca and Francesco would be away, I warned Petey and Tony, the two musclemen, that there might be another attempt to search the house that night. I was going onto the yacht to keep my ears open and learn what I could.

"Nobody'll get in this time," Petey assured me.

The house was very quiet. As I made my way up to my room, I saw Donna walking down the hall. She smiled and waved, so I yelled that I was going to take a nap and didn't want to be disturbed. I figured this was as good a time as any to check the contents of that third suitcase, the one the S.P.E.R.M. man had put on board the plane for me in Paris. Now I knew damn well that Bocca or Francesco, or maybe Donna at their orders, had searched all my luggage, and had found nothing to incriminate me.

This meant that S.P.E.R.M. had hidden the weapon—if there was any—very carefully, very cleverly. I had to be clever enough to find out where and what it was. There had to be a weapon, I reasoned: otherwise, that third valise made no sense at all.

I closed the bedroom door, went to the bureau drawer. Now Donna had helped me unpack, but the contents of the third valise I'd put away myself. Of course, Donna or one of the boys would have examined all the items, but I have almost a photographic memory, I could remember everything that had been in that suitcase.

So I went over them, one by one.

I found nothing.

It took me an hour and a half, actually, before my fingers, wandering idly along the lace fringe of a pair of black nylon panties, found the code. The stitching of the lace seemed odd, it did not quite match the pattern of the lace around the elastic band of the waist. I went over it more carefully.

The stitching was in code. Not Morse, but a brand of code that S.P.E.R.M. agents learn, it belongs to them alone. And the message read: C-h e-c-k-t-h-e-l-i-p-s-t-i-c-k.

My hand went to the Estee Lauder lipstick, it was a fairly large one. I examined it closely, it was not dissimilar from other lipsticks I'd seen at S.P.E.R.M. school. My lip salve part was real enough, but it was hollowed out to hold a thin barrel. The base was a cleverly contrived airgun that would shoot something lethal into whatever or whoever I aimed it at when I twisted the base.

Cyanide pellets, probably. I didn't need to ask what it was, it would be damn deadly. I put the contents of the third suitcase back where they belonged, and began unraveling the stitching on the panties. No sense in leaving them around for somebody else to discover their message. The lipstick I hid among my nylon stockings.

Then I lay down to rest up for the evening's entertainment.

Donna was on hand to help me dress, asking questions about the yacht, the Countess and my banker friend. She laid out a blue-beaded blouse done in a fish-net style, and sheer organza trousers to match. You could see bare skin through the blouse and the trousers. Since nudity is all the rage along the Riviera, I would be right in style. I selected a pair of big Swan earrings to go with them.

Etienne Montaigne would positively drool when he saw me naked in that outfit, I told myself, turning slowly before the mirror. So would the Countess.

With evening pumps on my bare feet, I was ready when a Jaguar pulled up to the front door. A uniformed chauffeur was there, hand touching his peaked cap respectfully. Etienne Montaigne was waiting in the car for me, he told me.

I went down the few steps seeing my old goat spring out of the car and make a deep bow. He wore a black cloak that covered him from head to toes.

"Enchante," he exclaimed as he caught my hand

and kissed it.

As the car swept us through the lovely Saint Tropez night, I wondered how Bocca Carducci and Francesco Galuppo were making out with the don who ran the whole Mafia show. What would he say to the fact that a redhead had shown up at their house instead of Joe Turessi?

For all I knew, the boss of bosses might even then be ordering my execution.

Chapter Five

The party was getting into high gear as I put my evening pumps on the deck of the *Alsace*. A naked brunette, breasts swinging crazily, was running past the ladder with a naked young man in pursuit of her. His rigid manhood leaped and bounced to his strides as he sought to overtake her. Behind him, in the shadows, I saw a man and woman squirming their naked bodies together.

"Well," I said, "Things are under way already."

"These are the *sauvages*, those who cannot contain their animal desires, *ma cherie*," whispered Etienne, catching my elbow and guiding me aft.

"And we can?" I giggled

"So early in the evening, of course. But we must have them, for at the moment, these people are the true Tropezians, movie folk and artists of sorts, a writer or two. They are seen everywhere that is anywhere. They feel they add a certain flair to what-ever party they attend."

The Countess was waiting stark naked by the little bar set up for the evening. She had a damn nice shape, even if her belly paunched just a little. She ran up to me, hugged me, kissed me, stood back to admire the beaded blouse and organza trousers.

"So distinguished," she enthused. "Absolutely adorable."

Her black eyes studied the way my nipples peeped out of the holes in the fish-net beaded blouse. They roved downward to where my thighs joined and my red pubic hair made a splotch of color behind the blue organza. Her own nipples were up, thick and heavy.

"I feel I'm overdressed," I smiled, letting my own eyeballs do the grand tour over her body.

"Not at all. It adds mystery." She made a face, saying, "I—I am too much revealed, *n'est ce pas?*"

I played the game, I told her, "You are as the lily of the fields, *ma comtesse*, as mentioned in the bible. Who else can be arrayed as one of these?"

My hand touched her hip, ran up to her breast, lazily fondled it. There was lustfire in her eyes and her tongue came out to lick her lips. I don't know what would have happened if Etienne hadn't caught me and drawn me away. The Countess was ready for a bout of lesbian love.

Etienne dropped his cloak. Under he wore only *le*

minimum, that typically Rivieran garment that consists of a small vee of black cloth that covers the genitals. Now *le minimum* is an accepted garment in Saint Tropez. One goes anywhere in it—and it alone—if one feels like doing so and has the body to wear it. Etienne had a pretty good body for his age, but it did sag here and there.

I pretended enchantment. I laughed and lifted off the beaded blouse. My breasts were firm, solid. They'd hardened as the Countess had looked me over. My old goat grinned at the sight of them, bent to kiss the nipples.

"A drink first, cherie, *un dry* or a *cassis*. And then a swim, *non?*"

Un dry for me, a *cassis* for him.

Then he put his hands on my blue organza trousers and slid them downward. He knelt to slip off my evening shoes, and leaned to put his mouth into my red pubescence.

"We shall swim now," he nodded.

We stepped out onto the diving board attached to the ship boat deck and dove. The water was cool, refreshing. It was heavenly to swim here with the blue sky and the brilliant stars overhead, with the moon like a silver melon. It was a romantic setting. I found myself wishing it was Mark Condon naked in a minimum beside me rather than Etienne Montaigne. But sexterminators for S.P.E.R.M. can't be choosers. I had a job to do.

As we floated, with my breasts rising above the surface, I said casually to my banker friend, "Did you know robbers had broken into the house where I'm staying, last night?"

"I heard rumors," he admitted.

Now how had he found out? I knew gossip was in the air at Saint Tropez, but this was a little much. Neither Petey nor Tony nor Donna would spread the word. I was damn sure Bocca Carducci and Francesco Galuppo hadn't blabbed. And until now, I'd kept mum.

For the first time, my head sounded a warning.

Hey, now! Maybe Etienne Montaigne had engineered that housebreaking. The thought almost numbed me. He had money, he made protests at the idea of needing or wanting any more. But suppose he had a hankering for power? He could have hired thieves to search the house for that gadget.

I didn't know what the gadget was, but it must be damned important. Here I was, stark naked in the water and without a weapon to call my own, in case anybody played rough.

"They didn't get anything," I went on, lazily stroking. "I guess Bocca and Francesco don't keep large sums of money in the house. They must bank it with you, Etienne."

He was silent for a long minute. I think he was cursing himself for having inadvertently revealed the fact that he'd known about the robbery. Then he said, very lightly, "They do have accounts with my bank, I believe. They are very well-to-do business-men. They have an interest in a fishing fleet, I think."

Their fishing fleet would run drugs, no doubt.

"Shall we go back on board?" he asked softly.

"Why not? I'm hungry as a bear after its winter hibernation. Besides, I could go another *dry* to warm me up."

He came crowding his nakedness against mine. "I could warm you up, *ma petite*. Why not let me try?"

His hand was at my buttocks, caressing them as we drifted. "Why not?" I asked cheerily. "You were a perfect lover last night. Can you perform as well again tonight?"

"I shall be even better," he vowed.

The party was hitting on all cylinders as we came up dripping from the sea. The nudity was almost blinding in the electric lights that hung like Japanese lanterns from prow to stern. There was no false modesty among the guests. I saw the brunette who had been running from her boy friend as I came aboard, kneeling before him now, her red tongue lashing over his extended erection as he leaned against the rail, eyes closed, hips jerking slightly, every once in a while.

Naked men and women were dancing together to the strains of Electric Ladyland by Jimi Hendrix while others were coupling to that same rhythm.

One woman was sitting on the edge of a table with a man between her wideflung thighs, another was bent over, her hands grasping the brass rail of the afterdeck, as a youth in his late teens ploughed in and out of her vaginal tunnel.

"Hey, wow," I said.

Etienne pressed his nakedness to me, rubbing back and forth against my buttocks. His hands were sliding over my belly, down into my girlish fur.

"Look at that couple," he breathed.

The man was standing, the woman was upside down, her hands just above his knees for balance. Her legs were apart, draped over his shoulders while his head was buried between her quivering thighs. He was eating her while her mouth was sliding up and down on his rigid shaft.

"How'd you like to try it that way?" my old goat asked.

"Too athletic for my tastes. But as a variation— not bad."

The young man bulged with muscles. He bulged with more than muscles, too, I saw as his girl friend paused in her oral occupation to take a deep breath. He was built like a stallion.

"Let's go find a bed, my love."

That might not be a bad idea, I told myself, watching as the woman had enough of the air to feast on and settled down to her tithioscopic task. Her head went back and forth slowly, I could hear her moaning in pleasure as the young man buried his mouth deeper between her legs.

"I think I need a drink," I muttered. There was so much lovemaking going on around me, everywhere I looked I saw so many folks having futtering fun, my bod was responding to it.

My breasts were hard and there was a definite dampness that was not from the Mediterranean Sea where I'd been swimming, in my privacies. Etienne knew it, the lecher, his hands were all over me, gently sliding and caressing.

A naked girl bartender handed me a *dry*, poured out a *cassis* for Etienne who had his rising shaft glued to my buttocks. We drank, with Etienne looking over my shoulder at the carnal carryings-on and making comments in my shell-pink ear.

"That one's lasting too long," he said of a man driving in and out of his female partner. "He must be high on hasheesh. Hasheesh is an aphrodisiac, you know. Or it may be only Spanish Fly.

"That woman, there! What a pair of love jugs!"

"Ahh! Two little girls, having their jollies."

The two girls he indicated were not so little. They were well into their twenties, but they were lean, small, almost like young teenagers. Just to one side of them I saw the Countess, slightly glassy-eyed as she watched their jerking breasts and bouncing buttocks. From time to time she would put out a hand, run it over and between their sweat-slick bodies, then have a sip of her *cassis*.

Etienne caught me by the wrist. "Come, my love. I'll never be readier."

I glanced down, saw he had come all the way out of his minimum. His staff was standing up quite proudly, quivering in the Japanese-lantern light. I put fingertips to it, ran them up and down.

I remembered how Etienne had been quite garrulous in the villa room where we'd made love. I wondered if he'd be as talkative in a yacht bedroom.

We ran across the deck on bare feet, dodged between a number of bare-assed men and women playing gonad games. Out of the corner of my eyes, I saw the Countess turn her head and stare after us.

The main salon of the yacht was half full of characters engaged in a group orgy. There were at least a dozen assorted male and female bodies draped over the chairs and the blue wall-to-wall carpeting, the twin sofas pushed back against the walls which were half windows. Moans and groans and sobs of passion paced us between jerking bodies, thrusting bodies, and even bumping bodies.

"The Alsace sleeps ten people," Etienne panted as he shoved me into a narrow companionway. There was a door in the wall. He reached for it.

I half expected to see naked bodies on the bed, but when the electrics came on my eyes told me the bedroom was empty except for ourselves. I thought it was a little odd that nobody but nobody would be in a bed, there was so much lovemaking going on all over the ship, but I paid no never mind to that little warning voice in my head.

Etienne flung himself on me, kissing my breasts and grappling for my thighs. "Hey, wait," I yelped, as I went down on the floor with a thump.

There must have been octopus blood in that old guy, his hands were everywhere. He was caressing my breasts, making them even harder than they already were, and then his fingers were between my legs, diving into and sliding along my genital trench, finding my stiff clitoris and giving it a big play.

I was getting hotter by the second. I felt a little like an orchestra that Etienne Montaigne was conducting, but he was so deft, so accomplished a lover, that he had me panting in no time at all. I just had to be made love to, he'd toyed an obbligato on every last one of my erogenous zones.

Just the same, I did work for S.P.E.R.M.

He was slobbering over my nipples, his hands on my inner thighs and pushing them apart, when I finally got my tongue to working.

"How did you find out about the robbery, honey?" I asked.

He chuckled around my wet left nipple. "The comtesse told me. She hears everything, that one. Didn't I tell you so at her villa?"

"Oh, yeah. The blackmail bit. You did mention it."

I wanted to push him away, but he would not push. The man seemed to be made of iron, though to look at him you'd think he was the scrawniest, weakest male on the boat. He was between my legs in no time and driving forward, right on target. He went into me all the way and I must admit, his see-sawing activity felt pretty good.

But I had one weapon in my arsenal, at least.

My interior muscles tightened up on him, held his stiff penis as if in a vise. His hips went on jerking back and forth, but he didn't slide inside me, I was holding him too tightly.

"How could the Countess know, lovey?"

"Wha—what? *Ne me tormenta pas!* You're killing me. Let go, let go. I can't move."

"Tell me what I want to know, I wheedled, running fingernails down his back to his buttocks. I gave a little ripple with those constrictor cunnae muscles as he let out a moan of pleasure.

"Mamma can be nice," I promised, "if you tell her what she wants to know."

"I can't, my darling. I just can't."

I got the feeling, staring up at his frustrated face above me, that my old goat could answer any question I had to ask about the Countess, about her methods of learning local scandals. And for some reason, I didn't think he was afraid of Colette de Vaux.

Why wouldn't he talk, then?

I eased back, lying spread-eagled on the carpet, with my nipples pointing up at the ceiling, while he half-crouched, half-knelt above me. He was buried deep inside me. He couldn't have gotten away from my constrictor cunnaes unless I wanted him to. So I started applying some pudendal pressure.

I began milking him with those interior muscles. He gasped like a gaffed fish, mouth open and his eyes rolling in his head as I worked on him. The sensations must have been terrific, because his body jerked and flopped around on me as though there were a clockwork mechanism inside him that had gone haywire.

Both my bare feet were propped on the carpeting, letting me use my legs and my hips in a levering movement that swung him up and around.

In seconds he was yelling.

"Satre bleu! C'est coince! It's stuck inside you! My God, woman! What are you doing to me?"

I let my behind sink to the carpet, dragging him down on me. I whispered, "Come on, give. Tell me how the Countess found out. Were those men with the binoculars keeping an eye on Bocca and Francesco and me to make sure we wouldn't know about the robbery? Is that it? Does she have a private little army of spies who watch the guests she robs?"

His face was a contorted mask of frustration. I held him in my pudendal pincers, tight.

He nodded, torn between his need for completion and his apparent fear of *la comtesse*. I twisted my loins and he damn near screamed. He was so hot, he was helpless in my genital grasp.

"Tell me, Etienne. Tell me."

It was like a bit of humping hypnotism. His eyes glared down at me from his sunbrowned face, his hair was up every which way, and his lips were grotesquely writhing.

"Does she—blackmail you, too?" I breathed.

He nodded. *"Oui, oui.* She is very—powerful, that woman. She has—friends—all over. One never knows when one of her spies is—at the elbow. You understand?"

I eased up on him, letting him pump away. With a sob of pleasure, he did just that, slamming in and out of me as if his life depended on it. Maybe it did, because I think if I hadn't given him that body-wrenching, hip-bucking sexual relief, he might have had a heart attack.

For a few seconds he rammed into me, his flesh dissolving in a wash of what the French call *colle*. He shook and quivered like a mad thing. Then he collapsed on me.

"Bravo! Bravo!" cried a voice from the doorway.

The Countess was standing there, stark naked, smiling down at us. There was lust in her black eyes, her brown nipples were long and hard, and I thought I saw a trace of wetness on her inner thighs.

We stared at each other over the inert body of

the old goat.

"Well, hello," I smiled.

She smiled down at me, but not nicely.

My brain flashed a warning signal. How long had she been standing there? Had she heard me asking questions? Had she heard what Etienne said to me? I didn't put it past her.

I patted the banker on his shoulder and began sliding out from under him. There was something about her amused smile that told me I was in for trouble. Yet she never moved from the doorway.

"Did you learn all you wanted to know?" she asked.

"Just curious, that's all."

"Well, it really doesn't make any difference."

She stood aside and two sailors stepped past her into the cabin. They were husky brutes, with dark blue sweaters on their torsos, and tight drill pants belted at their slim middles. They walked toward me like cats.

"Hey, what is this?" I laughed.

"I don't like nosey people, honey. Take her, boys!"

They came for me together, which was a mistake. I dropped to my knees and dove up under one of them, lifting him and throwing him sideways into his fellow. I heard French swear words, then I was on my own feet and chopping down with the edge of my right hand—I can break a two inch plank with the edge of that hand—across the throat of the man I'd just flipped through the air. My hand landed with a satisfactory thud.

I heard the Countess squawk behind me.

I would have whirled on her, but the number two sailor was yanking out what looked like a Malay kris, with a curved steel blade that glittered in the cabin's overhead lights, so I decided to pay more attention to him than to the naked lady.

He came with that knife aimed for my belly.

I went backwards, doubling up so the blade missed my tender girl-girl flesh. At the same time I stabbed out with the fingers of my left hand—in the shape of a vee for victory sign—driving my red fingernails right at his eyes. I missed both eyes when he ducked, but I hooked the corner of one and blood spurted.

He snarled, *"Merde!"* and leaped.

I lowered my head and butted him in the face.

I heard cartilege crunch, and turning slightly, brought my right elbow up hard into his solar plexus. The wind went out of him in a shrill whoosh.

Burmese boxing is a rough, tough sport, so much so that until recently, it has been banned even in Burma. In a Burmese boxing bout, just about anything goes. You can use your head, your elbow, your feet or any other part of the body in an attack. There are rules to be obeyed, however. No eye gouging, no blows to the groin, and no biting or hair pulling.

By rights, there should be a *saing* or musical group to make the rhythmic sounds to which the fight proceeds. I had no orchestra, so I made music in my head.

I had been taught Burmese boxing by experts. I'd even won a few 'flags' at the sport. So I moved in on the number one man, who was staggering to his feet with a hand at the throat I'd clobbered, with supreme confidence.

My right foot came up fast.

My heel caught him flush on the jaw. Now the human leg is a lot more powerful than the arm, it has a lot more muscles. And I'd been shown how to deliver the 'high kick' by my Burmese master of the art, Byen Dhu. It seemed I could hear him shrilling at me now as I moved in for the kill.

Both sailors were just about out, but I added a knee-belt to my routine, just to make sure. They flew back against the cabin bulkhead and sprawled on the floor, unconscious.

I turned for the door. The Countess was gone, I could hear her shrieking as she raced down the companionway. My beaded blouse and blue organza trousers were on the deck, but I told myself I really didn't need them. I could go over the rail and swim for shore just as I was, mother naked.

My feet beat echoes along the companionway. Ahead of me and running through the living room was Colette de Vaux. I went after her, figuring that if

I stopped her from rousing the rest of the crewmen, I stood a good chance to make it to shore and safety.

"Au secours! Au secours!" she shrilled. "Help Help!"

She was at the companionway leading to the deck when I finally caught her. She packed just a mite too much poundage to make her a fast runner. As I've said, to grab an opponent by the hair is a no-no in Burmese boxing, but the hell with rules when I was fighting for my life.

My hands went into her thick mane of black hair and my fingers tightened. I dug in my heels and yanked. The Countess screamed in agony as my backward tug lifted her off her feet and sent her spinning away, heels over head across the salon.

I went after her, hands curved into claws.

Both my knees landed on her belly, drove her deeper into the carpet. Her eyes rolled in her head and she went limp as a dead fish.

"That was stupid, Cherry," I told myself. "I wanted to ask her some questions. But the hell with the questions, right about now."

A sound on the companionway swung me around. Two more bruisers were coming down the steps. They didn't hesitate, they ran right at me. Which tipped me off, of course, to the fact that my being invited onto this yacht was a set-up to get me in the hands of *la comtesse*. Otherwise, the boys would have asked questions. I was their meat, their eyes told me so. I'd been their target, actually, ever since I'd set feet on the deck of the *Alsace*.

They were just as arrogant as the other two sailors had been. They saw a stark naked dame in front of them without a weapon, so they moved right in. I went to meet them.

A yard from them, I brought my right foot up. It was the old Burmese boxing high kick, and it landed smack-dab on the mouth of my target. He stopped in his tracks, stared at me in vast surprise, and made a gurgling sound in his throat.

His companion cursed and reached for me.

My hands came up, caught his wrist. I pivoted on bare toes, caught him across my hip, and flipped him upside down through the air. He landed on a table, the table legs gave way and he went down in a cloud of splintering wood.

Me, I ran for the companionway.

I came up on a deserted deck. The guests were all gone. Were they in on the conspiracy too? It made no never mind to me. I sprinted straight for the railing. I put two hands on the top rail and swung myself up and over.

The waters of the bay were right below me, moonlight gleaming on their surface. They seemed to reach up for my hurtling body. An instant later I was down there in the cool darkness, letting myself go down, down.

Then I began to swim.

I did the Australian crawl as fast as my arms and

legs could take me, across that water toward the beach. I made damn good time, something told me I was swimming for my life.

I was a few hundred yards away from those sands when I heard the tender motor. My head turned. The Chrysler Courier was sliding away from the *Alsace*, I could make out three men crouched in it. Then a floodlight came to life.

That blazing beam flashed across the waters.

It—touched me.

I dove, but I was too late. They'd seen my bare legs and feet as I went down. The whirring propellors made a tinny sound in the water that grew louder and louder in my ears.

Damn! I could have wept with frustration.

It was only a couple of hundred yards to the shore, but I might as well have been two hundred miles. The tender was overtaking me fast. And I needed to surface to breathe.

My lungs were bursting. I had to go up, I must take the chance. If I didn't, I'd damn well drown. The boat was almost overhead. It was a long black shape in the glare of its flashlight. But I had to have air. I plopped to the surface, drew a deep breath.

"There she is!"

"Arretez! Arretez! Stop!"

Something fluttered through the air.

Too late, I saw it was a net.

I dove, but the net was sweeping downward. It

caught my thrashing feet and slid up my legs. I tried to free myself of it. I doubled up and fought those tangling strands. I was wasting precious time and oxygen, I told myself, but the netman was twisting the handle in his hands and this made those meshes like fingers gripping and holding my ankles.

I came up again, sobbing for breath.

"Damn you," I howled, and caught the metal rim of the net. I tried to pry it free of the hands that held it, hoping to take it down under with me and free myself out of sight of the three sailors.

"I'll get her," said one of the men.

He came over the moldboard almost on top of me. His arms went around me, his hands caught hold of my water-slicked breasts and squeezed. Hard! The pain was excruciating. I tried to bite his hands, but he shifted them too fast for me.

One of the other two leaned over the side of the boat and brought an oar down across the top of my skull.

I saw all the stars in the firmament.

My body sagged a little, and the man who held me got a better grip. At the same time the netman pulled upward. I came out of the water feet first, still struggling, but only half conscious.

"She's a goddamn wildcat," said a man.

"*Merde!* If she could make love like she fights, I'd be tempted to sneak her away from the Countess."

"I can, I can," I mumbled but they didn't hear me.

I was just about beat. My body ached all over. I didn't even protest when they disentangled me from the net and handcuffed my wrists behind my back. Then they dropped me full length on the floor of the tender and stood there staring at me.

They were pretty well battered, these three. One had a broken nose that was still bleeding, another had lost some teeth. The third man had a purple bruise on his jaw the size of a chicken's egg. They had other bruises, I knew, but these were the ones that caught my eye.

To my surprise, they didn't start beating on me out of revenge. I must have bruised their male egos as well—the Countess had hired them as muscle-men, and a mere girl had just about put the quietus on them—but there was respect and a grudging admiration in their faces, just as there had been that same admiration in Francesco Galuppo's eyes when I'd tossed him over that chair.

They even grinned at me, friendly like. One said, "I am sorry for you, *joli morceau*. The Countess is very angry. You threw her about five feet through the air."

A second grinned. *"Oui!* She has bumps and bruises, too."

"And she is not a nice one to give bumps and bruises to, you bet. She will have it in for you."

Didn't I know it!

I lay there and told myself this was the end of the

road. It made no difference whether Bocca Carducci and Francesco Galuppo found out about me, now. I was in the clutches of *la comtesse*, and my instinct told me that was not a nice place to be, not at all.

"What do we do now?" I wondered.

"We take you to her, *ma cherie*. And fast!"

The motors rumbled to life. One of the sweatered men went to the helm, swung the tender around and headed it back toward the *Alsace*. I lay there and sweated. The woman named Colette de Vaux was going to torture me. I knew what the Countess wanted of me. All I had to tell her was what the gadget was that Bocca Carducci and Francesco Galuppo were going to hand over to me for delivery to Joe Turessi. Or where it was hidden.

And—

I didn't know the answer to either question.

Chapter Six

Colette de Vaux had put on a pair of black hip-huggers and a tight black jersey, I saw as she came down the ship's ladder and into the tender. She came slowly, carefully, her body was experiencing a few aches and pains right about now. One of the sailors held up his hand, she caught it and dropped into the boat.

She drew a deep breath, staring at me. Hate glistened in her eyes as she ran them over my helpless nudity. "I will take pleasure in this," she hissed. "Never have I been so humiliated."

Her hand made a gesture and the sailor with the broken teeth came and draped a tarpaulin over me. I felt the boat drift away from the *Alsace*, heard the motors start up. The boat swung around and headed for shore.

We were halfway there when a corner of the tarp

was thrown back and the Countess knelt there, staring down at me coldly. I saw a hypodermic needle in her hand.

She caught my left arm, twisted the flesh, jabbed me.

Whatever was in the syringe was potent. I blacked out.

Just before consciousness faded, I told myself that they would trundle me like a dead body wrapped inside the tarpaulin, dump me into a car and carry me....

My eyes opened on cold stone. I hung in chains, I saw, lifting heavy eyelids and staring around me. My naked behind was pressed against something hard and damp, and my legs dangled toward a stone floor. I moved my head back and forth, seeing sunlight coming in through a barred, narrow window. A rat was crouched a dozen yards away, eyeing me with its beady little eyes. I moaned and shifted my position, and the rodent fled.

There was a solid stone floor under my feet. The chains and manacles that held me were brightly polished, and seemed brand new. I could see other chains, other manacles on the walls of this dungeon, but those others were rusted with age and long disuse.

A door opened. Feet sounded on a wooden staircase.

One of the sailormen came into view. He carried a tray in a hand that he put on a wooden table. He pushed the table toward me. Then he lifted out a key and unlocked my right manacle.

"You can feed yourself," he told me.

He turned and went away.

When I whisked away the napkin covering the plates, I saw a platter of scrambled eggs and ham, some toast and a pot of coffee. Whatever the Countess intended for me, she wasn't going to starve me to death. It was awkward eating with the one hand, I had to stretch to reach the table and the plastic spoon that was the only utensil I was allowed. Maybe they thought I'd kill myself with anything stronger, like a knife or a fork.

Still, I really enjoyed that meal. I hadn't eaten the night before, all I'd had were those martinis. My stomach was empty and that breakfast tasted like nectar of the gods. So I'd be strong enough to stand torture, but I had to eat. And the coffee, surprisingly enough, was good. The French like the English, are not renowned as coffee makers.

When everything was gone and I still hung in that manacle about my left wrist, I took stock. I tried to wriggle free of the lone chain that held me, but it was no use. I was a prisoner, but good.

Then the door opened again and the sailor came downstairs. Following him was *la comtesse*, done up in a striped cotton jersey and matching hiphuggers. She stood back as the sailor locked my right wrist back in the other manacle, and watched while he dragged away the table. He took the platter with the empty plates and pot and went up the stairs. The Countess seated herself on the edge of the table, crossed her ankles and began swinging her feet back and forth.

"You are a member of the Family, my dear," she said softly. "You are an American. You are here on the Riviera—why?"

I smiled at her.

Her plucked black eyebrows rose. "Don't want to talk? Too bad. It will mean I must find ways to make you. As you've probably guessed by this time, you're in the cold cellars of my villa.

"Nobody will hear your screams when my men begin to work on your soft flesh. At one time, this place was a medieval castle. I have the suspicion that, before that, it was a Roman fort. These cellars were part of that fort. It was here that the Romans tortured the Gauls, and later on the medieval baron tortured his foes and sometimes his own peasants, just for the sport of it."

She smiled at me quite affably. "Now I'm not a sadist. I don't enjoy seeing another human being suffer—not as you will suffer, at any rate, my dear. But I am a business woman. I love money. I enjoy the feel of pounds, of dollars, of new francs, of lira.

"And you mean money to me."

"Me? I haven't a cent in the world," I protested.

The Countess laughed. "Very rich, your humor.

No, no, my love. It isn't your money I'm after. It's what's locked inside that head of yours."

My eyes got big. "And what's that?"

As if I didn't know! But I wanted to hear her spell it out for me. She fastened her black eyes on me and shook her head.

"You came from New York, darling, to visit Bocca and Francesco. Now I happen to know that those boys are very high in the Mafia. They certainly didn't send all the way to the United States for a little sexual amusement, though I know you're very good at that sort of thing.

"No, they had another reason.

"My gossips tell me that reason is an instrument, a thing, a gadget which you are to take back to New York with you. I want to know what it is—and where it is."

She leaned forward, eyes glinting. "Then it does exist?"

I shrugged. "So I've been told."

"Ahhh," she exclaimed. "That's what I wanted to hear. You do know about it. So now you can't profess to tell me you don't know where it is—or how I can lay hands on it."

"Look, Countess, Bocca and Francesco went to get it. I don't know who has it, or what it is. I'm assuming the boss of bosses has it in his possession. I'm to be given this gadget to take back to my *capo*. I can't tell you any more than that."

She showed her white teeth in a grin. "We'll soon know about that. Guy! Rollo!"

Two sailormen came down the stairs, only they were stripped to their middles and wore what looked to be purple pants, very tight. I guess the nakedness above their belts was to impress and even scare me with their hairy musculature. My eyes went over them, kept watching them as they came to stand on either side of Colette de Vaux.

Her hand waved at me. "She is yours, *messieurs*. I want to learn what she knows about a gadget presently in the hands of those two Cosa Nostra *capos* in the house on the Rue Bravade. When she is ready to talk to me, to tell me what she knows, do not torture her any more, but call me."

Her black eyes lingered on my nakedness as she shook her head. "It is too bad. I do not like to see such beauty spoiled. See what you can do to make her speak without deforming her, boys."

I shivered. She was so damn calm about it!

Guy and Rollo nodded. Guy was the man with the busted nose, Rollo was the sailor I'd caught across the mouth. His front teeth were missing, but there were bandages across his lips. A corner of my brain told me these boys had a score to settle with me. I could read nothing in their eyes, or on the faces that seemed like stiff masks of hard flesh.

Something also told me they would be good at their trade. The Countess did not keep incompetents about her. They waited until the Countess had ascended the wooden staircase before they made their move. It was as if the closing of the door above that stairs was the signal that put them into motion.

They moved together, as though they'd talked over what they would do to me. They came up to where I hung helpless, naked in those chains, and each man bent his head and ran his tongue over my breasts. I fought against the pleasure, but my bod is too conditioned to erotic excitement for me to be like wood in the face of such an attack. My nipples got big, they stuck up like huge reddish-brown erasers, and I had to fight to choke back my moans of pleasure.

Their mouths zeroed in on those nipples.

They suckled my tits for long moments while I writhed back and forth, the chains clanking a little. My inner thighs rubbed together. I could feel the dampness, the arousal of my private parts.

They put their hands on my thighs and stroked them, they moved their palms up and down my side. One dipped fingers between my thighs that I tried to press together, another reached behind me and after fondling my buttocks, ran his finger deep inside me in that caress the French know as *faire postillon.*

"No," I whimpered. "Please, no."

I had it all figured out, in my head. They were going to pleasure me—and then put the pain to me.

Use my emotions as a pendulum, first the pleasure, then the pain, until I would damn near go mad from frustration.

"You got some body, lady," said broken-teeth.

"It's fun to play with it like this!" laughed the other.

It *was* fun, too! Despite my helpless condition, my flesh thrilled to their strokings, their hungry suckings and the movements of their hands and fingers. I quivered with desire, helpless in the manacles. Then they drew back and grinned at me.

They were happy boys. I could measure the extent of their happiness by looking at the big bulges in the front of their purple pants.

One man rubbed me on the left, the other on the right as they put their hands to the manacles and unlocked them. I was too weak to fight them, the blood had run down out of my arms, just about. I needed to massage them to put any strength back into the muscles.

They didn't give me the chance for that. A hand touched a lever and two more manacles attached to long chains came down from the ceiling. The men lifted me, fitted my ankles into them. I hung upside down, still naked.

Guy—the sailor with the busted nose—chuckled as he went to the stone wall and pulled another rod. The chains moved apart—wide apart—and took my legs with them. I was upside down now with my wet pussy exposed to their eager eyes.

Guy said, "You go first, Rollo."

Rollo lifted a big feather with a lot of fluffy fronds to it and began tickling the insides of my legs. He went all the way down my inner thighs and then drew those strands across my wet femininity.

I howled, the torture was so exquisite.

Oh, I was in no pain. Just the opposite, in a way. The teasing tickle of that feather was out of this world. If Rollo was going to throw himself on me and take me in a little while, I was all for what he was doing. But—no such luck. This was just part of my punishment.

Because when Rollo was finished, in about ten minutes, Guy stepped into view. He held a switch in his hand, of peeled willow sticks bound together with leather thongs to form a handle.

He took his stance behind me, staring down between my legs. I must have been wet and open, I knew my clitoris was standing up, the sight of my *con* would have put iron in a lump of dough.

Guy was no lump of dough. He had one big erection.

Then—

The willow switch came down across my genital gash.

I screamed. I shook in those chains, trying to double up and put my hands to my stinging, smarting privacy. As I started to do so, Guy stepped back and let me have the switch across my hanging breasts.

I did some more screaming, thumping in the chains.

This went on for quite a little while, back and forth on my genitals and my breasts, until I was half mad with agony. Guy and Rollo were half mad too, but with the need to satisfy the swollen shafts making tents out of their purple pants' fronts.

"Why don't you boys have a little fun?" I found myself gasping through the sobs my throat was making.

"We are having fun," Rollo grinned.

"You could have even more, if you'd think about it," I panted. "I'm damn near helpless. You could have me, this way. Come on, fellas. How about it? You've got me so worked up, I'm climbing the walls."

They looked at each other, and glanced at the staircase. The door above it remained shut. There was indecision on their faces, so I coaxed them a little with, "Go tell the Countess I won't talk yet, but you have hopes. Tell her to give you another hour and I'll break."

Rollo nodded, ran for the stairs.

I said to Guy. "Lower me a little more. I'm up too high for you, this way."

He ran for the lever on the wall, moving it to bring me down so that I could rest the back of my neck on the stone floor. It wasn't comfortable, but it would have to do. When Rollo came running back, I was all ready for a good rape.

"The Countess is going into town," he panted. "We got maybe two whole hours." He stared hard at me. "This isn't some kind of trick, is it?"

"What trick?" I asked, half on my back with the legs up there in the air, held invitingly apart by the chains. "What in hell do you think I can do, except get jazzed?"

"Nobody'll know," grinned Guy, beginning to shuck out of his purple pants. He was stiff as a steel rod, and very proud of his erotic endowment. He had reason to be.

"Me first," Rollo growled, pushing down his own trousers to reveal himself in a state of extreme male want. If anything, he was even bigger than Guy. He was like a goddamn bull in rut.

"Hey, don't hurt me," I said. "You two boys are awfully big."

"You can take us, honey. You're damn wet."

Well, I was wet, but some of it was blood they'd drawn with that switch. I didn't say anything, but I was thinking hard as Rollo came between my bare legs, caught hold of the underslopes of my thighs, and drove himself forward. He went in deep, it was like taking a stallion. I whimpered, I shouted, as he rammed in and out of me.

"Lower the chains a little more," I begged Guy. "I

want to wrap my legs around him."

Guy did what I asked and then came running back to watch, tongue out and running around his lips. I was sliding up Rollo by this time, my legs were wrapped about his lean hips and we were both sawing away at each other like metronomes gone mad. By the time I finally got to Rollo's throat, I flung my arms about his shoulders and used them to help myself pump up and down on him.

He was yelling in delight, his hips bucking, thrusting, stabbing. Sweatbeads rolled down his face. His eyes were rolling around like marbles on a tilt machine and his lips were twisted grotesquely.

I turned my head and smiled at Guy who was just about going crazy, watching the action but not getting any of the goodies. He was actually suffering, he kept biting his lip and shaking, and from time to time his hand went down to where he was suffering the most.

"Ever hear of doing it *peche philosophique?*" I breathed.

His eyes nearly bulged from his head as he ran his stare down to my bouncing buttocks. I'm not in favor of this backdoor bumfiddling, but I was in a mighty, desperate fix. I had to get away from this dungeon, all in one piece. And the only way I'd been able to think of doing it was. . . .

"*Oui,*" breathed Guy, stepping behind me.

His hands caught my buttocks, parted them. I felt

him attack, grunted and sobbed to its momentary pain, because Rollo wasn't stopping to let his friend mount me. He kept hammering away harder than ever which made it more difficult for Guy. But with determination and a savage disposition that didn't care how much he hurt me while he was doing it, he finally got himself seated.

They went at it hammer and tongs.

Well, naturally, I got my come-uppances too. I was having myself a ball with both of them, bouncing up and down, trying to rouse them to that degree of sexual heat known as *se sentir des velleites* in which nothing but the satisfaction of the senses counts. The house could burn down around the head, but the *droit d'hymen* must be completed, at all costs!

I wriggled my breasts against Rollo's hairy chest. I turned and threw a bare arm about Guy, fastening my open lips to his. I swapped tongue tappings with him, hooking his neck with my right arm while my left was around Rollo's throat. In this position I was twisted out of the way for what was to come.

I tickled their necks with my fingernails.

Then I bent my fingers around their necks, slid them up to the backs of their heads. I paused a moment, tightened my sphincter and my constrictor muscles on what they held in their grasp.

I drove my hands toward each other.

Since I held their heads in my hands and since

they were half out of their skulls with pleasure, I don't think either sailor knew what was happening until their foreheads cracked together. Almost in the same movement, as they drew back in astonished reflex, I drove the edge of my right hand into Rollo's throat, then swung about and slammed it into Guy's Adam's apple.

They went down in a heap. I didn't go quite so far, there were still chains around my ankles. But half of me fell with them and I used my hands to ferret out the keys to my manacles from Rollo's pocket.

I doubled up, caught a chain, and used the key.

It was just the work of another second to free my other leg. I sank onto the stone floor in a half-faint, exhausted. My mind whispered to me that I didn't have the time to lie here and let lassitude ooze all over me. I had to get up and get the hell out of this place.

I paused to drive their skulls into the stone floor to make sure they slept on for a time. Then I raced, naked as the day I was born, for the staircase. Luckily, the door wasn't locked. I opened it and peered into an empty hall. I recognized the villa hall; when I'd been there last, this place had been lined with chairs and divans on which folks had been making love.

My bare feet took me down the hall and out the front door into the sunlight. There was a delivery truck off to one side of the drive, evidently a local wine shop was replenishing the *comtesse's* cellar. I went for that truck as a cat goes for catnip.

The key was in the ignition, the motor was running.

Three seconds later I was barreling along the drive, crouched over the steering wheel and blessing the delivery man, whoever he might be. I skidded and careened along the narrow roads like a drunk German driver, than whom there is no worse. But what did I care? I was free. Free!

I came down into Saint Tropez with a squeal of brakes and a joyous thudding of my heart that told me I was home free. I made for the Rue Bravade and when I saw the house where I was staying, I damn near wept.

I was out of the car and up the stone steps in nothing flat. My fist banged on the door until Petey opened it. His eyes got big at the sight of me, he was so surprised he didn't step back, so I had to push him out of the way to get inside.

"Has Bocca come back yet? Or Frankie boy?" I panted.

Bocca came to the archway between the hall and the front room, cool and suave in an Emilio Pucci suit with a Dior tie that showed off his blonde good looks. I ran for him, flung myself into his arms. His arms closed around me as his voice made little soothing sounds.

"Easy, *stellina!* Nothing's going to hurt you."

"Nothing now, no. But for a while there. . . ."

The story poured out of me, the words flowing like tones of water when a dam bursts. I explained how I'd gone to the yacht and how I'd fought for my life, how the sailors finally captured me in that net. . . .

"Bocca!" said a cold voice. "Bring the lady in here."

Bocca took off his coat and draped it about my shoulders before he turned me and brought me into the living room where a big, hard-faced man with blue jowls was chomping on a cigar and fastening his cold snake-eyes on me.

"Who's this?" he snorted.

Bocca explained and introduced me to Benito Castraccia. I guess my eyes popped a little. Benito Castraccia was the boss of bosses of the whole Mafia operation, a man so powerful in his way, if not more so, as the President of the United States or the Premier of the Union of Soviet Socialist Republics.

"So you're the girl from America," he grunted, finally.

"And you're in trouble. Bad trouble," I snapped.

Frankie goggled at me. "Cherry, this is the big man. The one."

"Well, somebody's out to cut in on your pie, then."

I picked up my story from the time they dragged me onto the tender until just a few minutes ago when I'd banged on the front door of this house to be let in.

"The Countess intends to get that gadget, whatever it is," I told him. "She sent me to rob the house while we were at her party. She was going to torture me to make me tell what it is and where it is. Fortunately, I didn't know. But that wouldn't have saved me from a painful death.

"She'd never have believed me!"

Benito Castraccia stirred his thick bulk. His little eyes went to Bocca and to Francesco. His teeth cut down on the cigar as if it were a personal enemy.

"The Countess! The Countess! How come you two didn't know about this woman? Hey? How come this hole from New York had to find it out, hey? I don't like it. I don't like it—not one little bit."

He scowled at me as if it were all my fault. I said, "How come she learned about the gadget at all? I thought it was a big secret!"

He nodded heavily, his dark jowls rippling. "It is a big secret. It was a big secret. I don't know how anybody found out." He looked at Bocca and at Francesco and they damn near wet their pants in fear. If the boss of bosses decided either one or both of them had played him false, they were very dead men in a very short time.

Bocca said, "Nobody knew. Nobody! Just us!"

"He's right, boss. Bocca's right!" chimed in Frankie boy.

"Then how come the Countess knew about it, hey? How come?"

Francesco looked at me. "Maybe the hole told her."

I spat, "Don't try to pass it off on me! She knew about it, that's why she set me up at that yacht party of hers. She had her buttons ready to go to work on me before the party was over. You think I'm crazy? If I so much as breathed a word of it to her, I'd have been signing my own death warrant.

"As it is—somebody else signed it."

The don chewed his cigar in silence, scowling. Finally he nodded. "That's what I want to know. Who spilled? Who got loose-tongued and let that dame know about it?"

I did a little fast thinking. If Benito Castraccia was here in Saint Tropez, that must mean the gadget was here, too. I planted my bare rump in a chair and crossed my equally bare gams as I scowled right back at the don.

"What is this gadget? Is it worth all the trouble I've been in? It better be!"

The don stared at me coldly. Then he chuckled, spilling cigar ashes all over his big chest and belly. "Is it worth her trouble? Is it worth her trouble? That's a good one." He leaned toward me.

"This thing's the biggest weapon we've ever had, that anybody's ever had," he exulted. "You ever hear of radio-hypnotic intercerebral control? Like where a doctor puts some electrodes into a man's brain and he has to obey the commands that a radio signal flashes to him?"

I vaguely recalled something of the sort. I said thoughtfully, "Doctor Delgado of Yale University has done some work in that field, hasn't he? It was theorized that may be why Oswald killed President Kennedy and why Ruby shot Oswald, because they were radio-controlled to do so."

The don gave a big grin. "You're pretty smart for a hole. You got it, lady. But the gadget goes a step beyond that. A mighty big step." He snapped his fingers. Francesco Galuppo moved to a table, opened a drawer, lifted out a wooden box. He put it almost reverently in the hands of the boss of bosses.

Benito Castraccia opened the box. He lifted out what looked like a big silver pencil, only instead of a point, the thing had a lens. He pointed it at Bocca Carducci. Bocca went rigid.

"You see?" Castraccia exulted. "He don't know nothing. Instant hypnotism is what I call it. It was invented by an Italian scientist—a man to rival Enrico Fermi himself. He did a lot of work on reflexology, he took the discoveries of other men, men like Delgado, Artemous, Vasiliev, and he did what they've been trying to do. Maybe they've even done it too, for all I know.

"But right now, as far as I can tell, this is the only radio control gadget of the human brain in existence." His hand lifted the thing, let me see it. "I can hypnotize anybody just by shining this light into his eyes. There's a radio beam working on the parts of his brain that control his emotions, his responses. Bocca!"

"Yes, sir?" answered Bocca in a normal voice.

"Kiss the girl's foot, Bocca."

Bocca knelt down, kissed my foot. My eyes touched Frankie boy. His face was as white as a piece of paper. I knew just by looking at him that Bocca was doing something he would have died rather than do if he'd known about it.

While Bocca was still slobbering over my foot, the don growled, "When I turn this thing off, he won't know what he did."

"It's devilish," I whispered.

"You bet it is, lady. Can you imagine what the Family can do with half a dozen of these things? A dozen? We can start a run on the stock market over in your country, buy when stocks are low, then make people—heads of mutual funds, big businesses, banks and other investors—buy and buy, force the price of our stocks up. We can sell out and make ourselves a billion dollars. Any time we want.

"Or we can make generals turn over secrets of the Pentagon to us so we can sell them to foreign agents. We can make judges free our boys even when the testimony is all against them. We can start wars— and end them. We can rule the world with this.

"The beauty of the thing is, we don't need no electronic thing inside a guy's head to make him obey. Just a shot or two of the light and the radio signal and he's our meat."

He leaned back and kissed the thing.

I stared at it in horror.

I told myself if I had to get it away from Benito Castraccia and the others, somehow there must be a way for me to lay my hands on it and . . . hey, now. Wait up. I remembered all of a sudden that the don was going to give this gadget to me to take to Joe Turessi. That's why I was here.

I sat up straight. "You mean to tell me you're going to turn that thing over to me to take back to Joe? What's he going to do with it?"

The don chuckled. "Have a dozen of 'em made. Have two dozen, three dozen. We got smart boys in the United States. Engineers, metallurgists, working for the Family. This has been a long time coming, but now we got it. And we're going to make lots of these—and see that nobody else lays hands on it."

"But—why me? Something so important! I'm a little speechless. I could take it somewhere, sell it."

"You won't go alone, lady. Some of my boys will be with you every step of the way. You see, Joe knows you. He trusts you. Joe also has the right contacts with the brain boys in the Family, over on your side of the ocean. You take the gadget to Joe, my boys go with you to make sure you do, and Joe turns it over to the brains. We'll have buttons watching Joe as well as the brains. We don't want no copies made that don't belong to us.

"Say one of the brain boys decides to make an extra one and sell it. He just won't be able to do it without us learning about it. The guy dies, then. Not nicely. No. It'll take him a long time going. Teach the other boys a lesson."

He grinned at me like a big fat toad.

That was when the doorbell rang.

I knew the doorbell was danger. Nobody needed to tell me. My feminine intuition was sending the message all along my nerve ends.

Chapter Seven

The man who came into the salon with Petey was small and lean, vulpine in appearance, with large teeth and small ears that seemed to cling to the sides of his head. His black eyes touched me, fell away. He was dapper, neatly turned out in a pinstriped suit and boldly checked tie against a dark blue shirt. He gave Benito Castraccia a faint smile almost by an effort of will. He was not a happy man, I thought.

"Ricco," nodded the boss.

"Just got back, I was in America," the little man said softly.

"Well? What about it?" asked Bocca.

The dapper man flashed me a grim look. "She took off on the night Guiseppe Turessi died."

I made myself say, "What's that? Joey's dead?"

"He died in the funeral home. One of the boys found him lying in a coffin—naked."

Benito Castraccia sat up straighter, scattering ashes from his cigar. "Naked? What was he doing in a coffin naked? Did—how did he die?"

"Heart attack."

There was a little silence, in which everybody glared at me. I spread my hands and looked helpless. "Don't look at me. When I left him, he was in great spirits."

"He'd been entertaining a hole," went on the little man. "That's what was on the police blotter. We got lawyers working on it. They're trying to find out how he died—and who might have killed him."

The boss of bosses rolled the cigar around between his lips while he considered me. "He was entertaining a woman, you say. He was—naked. So, then. Perhaps the excitement of his lovemaking may have proved too much for his heart. Is that the way the *polizza* figure it?"

"Yes, sir."

"Did you make love to him before you flew here?" Castraccia asked me.

"No, I didn't."

The boss of bosses smiled grimly. "Bocca tells me you make love very well. It might be that you were too—kind—to Joe Turessi. In which event, he might easily have had a heart attack."

"But who would have put him in a coffin?"

He smoked a few more puffs worth. He nodded heavily. "Yes. This puzzles me. I am not satisfied with what I have learned. It makes a difference."

His hand went out to the wooden box and the thin silver thing it held. His thick fingers that seemed more used to a pickhandle than to touching such a delicate instrument, lifted it as he turned the lens in my direction.

"I can find out what I want to know," he said softly. "With this. You're going to spill your guts, girl, when I shine this on you. I'll be able to get to the bottom of—"

That was when the gunshot sounded.

Glass broke. Something tore away half the cigar the boss of bosses was chewing, shredded it and sent chunks of tobacco flying this way and that. I sat there paralysed. For a brief second I thought maybe Frankie boy or Bocca had gone nuts, had lifted out a rod and begun blasting away with it.

The don snarled, "What the hell!"

He dove for the floor a half second after I did. We lay there with the box between us while Frankie and Petey went running to the windows, their Walthian Berettas in their hands.

"It's some of our own boys," Frankie gasped. "I know 'em. There's Little Louie and Charley and Boob and Fat Sam. . . ."

There were more gunshots. Now Frankie and Petey were firing back. The don stared coldly into my face, about five inches from his own.

"I'm going to work on you, baby," he snarled,

"When I get rid of them others. Bocca! What the hell are you doing, just standing there?"

"You hypnotized him with the gadget," I reminded him.

"Oh! Oh, yeah!"

His hand still held the gadget, that he'd been about to use on me. Instead he turned it, focussed it on Bocca Carducci. The blonde man stirred, shook his head, looked around a little dazedly.

The don snapped instructions. Bocca bent and lifted me to my feet. The don said, "Lock her upstairs in her room. Then start firing on them guys. The nerve of them!"

"They want the gadget," I yelled back as Bocca tugged me toward the hall staircase. "The Countess knows you'd bring it yourself. She must have had men watching the house the way she had them watching us with binoculars at her party."

The don pulled a German Lugar automatic from a shoulder holster. His face was dark with congested blood, with fury. He ran toward one of the windows.

I said to Bocca as we went up the stairs, "Look, I can help you. I'm reasonably good with a gun."

He smiled and shook his head. "Not without the don's say-so, honey. Now be a good girl and get in your room and stay there. We can handle those punks."

I went into my room, watched as he closed the door and locked it. I told myself I was a dead girl if I stayed in this room. I was also a dead girl if I tried to get out through that door. Bocca would shoot me without any compunctions if I tried it.

I ran to my bureau, yanked open a drawer. Seconds later my hand closed around the false lipstick that would shoot cyanide pellets or whatever, when I twisted its base. I put it on the bureau, then reached for my wired bra. A pair of panties, the black nylons my fellow S.P.E.R.M. agent had put into my luggage, a tan pullover sweater and beige slacks completed my outfit. I debated between pumps and sneakers, then settled for the Keds. I was going to have to move fast, when I did make my move.

Then I went to the window.

I could see down into an alleyway where some trash cans and refuse bags lined the walls. I looked up, saw the eaves of the red-tiled roof. By lowering the window and standing on it, I could reach that roof.

I slid out, standing on the six-inch stone window ledge that ran around this wall of the house. I clung to a brick with one hand and lowered both halves of the window. I put feet on the lowered sashes, reached up. My fingertips brushed the eaves.

I swore under my breath, took a deep breath and leaned back to study the rest of the windows. There was a window to my left, higher than mine. From there, I could surely reach the roof.

I lowered myself gingerly to the six-inch ledge

and began moving out on it. I was almost at the other window, which was partly open, when I heard the sound of a door closing. My heart damn near stopped. If Bocca was in that room, he would come to the window and peer out at the alleyway below in search of rebellious members of the Family.

I waited, but there was no Bocca, no sound. Carefully, I leaned to my left, peered in the window.

Benito Castraccia was in the room, kneeling before a little safe set into the wood paneling of the lower half of the wall. He was lifting out the thin rod that was his instant hypnotizer, putting it into the safe.

My hand went to my slacks pocket.

In front of me was the boss of bosses of the entire Mafia operation. Not only that, but in his hand was the gadget that might mean the difference between freedom for the western world or slavery to these crime lords.

My left leg slid into the room.

I posed like that, raised the lipstick and took aim. I twisted the base and there was a faint popping sound, like pent-up air suddenly released.

Benito Castraccio grunted and leaned forward. For a moment he rested like that with the silvery gadget in his left hand and his right palm pressed against the wooden half-wall to help him maintain his balance.

He turned his head slowly, stared at me.

I think he was dying, even then, but he let the hate and the rage come up into his eyes as they locked with mine. "You," he whispered. He fought the agony and the coming death in his flesh to turn, to raise himself and face me. His left hand dropped the radio-control gimmick and reached for the Luger in his shoulder holster.

"Damn you to hell," he breathed.

I leaped from the window, sped across the room. I dove for him, my shoulder catching him above his belt-buckle, even as my hands closed on his gun wrist. We fought for that Luger, he and I, silently and hardly breathing.

The reason he didn't yell, I believe, was that he was a man, filled with the male pride that just wouldn't let him cry out for assistance against a girl. He was a beefy man, given over to fat now, but there had been a lot of strength in him at one time. There was enough strength still left in him, because he swung me out and away from him with what seemed like a flick of his arm.

"I'll kill you slow for this," he breathed.

I let go of his gun, chopped at his neck.

The edge of my hand landed on his Adam's apple. His eyes bulged, his mouth opened, and he gurgled blood. At least, blood came into his throat and dribbled from the corners of his lips. Now he couldn't yell for that help he so desperately needed; he tried, mouth wide open, but he made only a mewing sound.

I brought my knee up into his crotch.

The don went white. He took a staggering step, eyes filled with pain, and then he fell forward.

I caught him, not wanting the thud of his heavy body to alert the house. I lowered him on the floor, where he writhed in agony. I stood there, looking down at him, waiting for his convulsions to stop. Then I bent and picked up the silver rod, staring down at it. It was thin, a trifle long. I didn't dare go running around on rooftops with it in my pocket, it might fall out. Almost absently, I picked up the Luger automatic, shoved it into my slacks belt.

I had to hide the hypnotic rod, and fast.

There was no need to worry about the boss of bosses any more. He lay quiet. I felt certain he was dead, or so near death from the poisoned pellet I'd put into him that it made no never mind.

I put my hands to my tan jersey and started lifting it off over my head. I had a hiding place for that rod, after all. A few moments later I started moving toward the window, yanking the jersey down over my red hair. That was when the door opened a second time.

I whirled, lifting the Luger.

Donna was standing at the door, staring at the dead body of Benito Castraccia, then letting her big eyes bug at me.

"Get in here—and close that door!" I snapped.

She did what I told her, half fainting. She leaned her back against the door and whispered, "You killed him. You killed the don, the boss of bosses!" It was as if she were reciting a litany.

"Look, Donna. I don't want to hurt you, but I can't leave you here to spread the word."

She gave me a friendly smile. "Me? Tell Bocca and the others? Hardly! But what are you going to do?"

"I'm getting out of here—fast."

"But how?"

I jerked my head at the window. "Up on the roof. What bothers me is, what am I going to do with you?"

"Take me with you," she breathed.

I started to laugh, but she was serious. Tears came into her eyes, she clasped her hands and went down on her knees.

"Please, I beg. I plead, lovely lady! Take me with you to America. Ahhh, if only you could! Please!"

"I don't know, Donna. If the others see us, there's going to be fighting. You might get hurt."

"Marrone! Do you think I cannot fight? I will do anything to get away from here. The Family is not what is once was, here. There are factions—many factions, all fighting. I am afraid. Very afraid."

She was still on her knees begging, hands clasped and fat tears running down her cheeks. Well, hell. I guess I could take a chance. "All right, come on. But no funny stuff. I'm uptight enough as it is. At the first sign of some treachery, Donna—I'll kill you."

She nodded, smiling happily, getting to her feet.

"I'll go first," I told her, "And make sure the coast is clear. You come after me, *capisce?* If I can, I'll help pull you up on the roof."

I stepped onto the ledge. Donna lowered the windows, guided my foot up onto the sashes. I reached for the roof, tightened fingers around a lead gutter and gently put my weight on it. My feet came free of the window sashes.

For a few seconds, I hung there above the alley.

My muscles tightened, I started pulling myself up. In another few seconds, I was hooking a knee over the leader, grabbing for a red tile and pulling myself the rest of the way.

I gulped in air, lying on the tiles, until I felt strong enough to slide to the edge and look over. Donna was coming out of the window, putting a foot on the sashes, stretching her arm up toward me. I caught her hand, guided it to the leader.

She was trying to pull herself up, my hands went to her wrists and tugged. It was hard work, I had no firm purchase on which to set my feet, so it was tug and puff, strain and pant, until finally I managed to hook her knee and slide it onto the leader.

Donna hung there, flushed and sobbing for breath. One of her legs was hanging free, the other was cocked over the eaves of the roof. If anybody had been in that alleyway, he'd have had a fine look at her crotch.

We could hear the sound of gunshots, the shouts of men who'd been hit by bullets. Footsteps pounded along the pavements at the front of the house.

"Can you make it?" I gasped.

She nodded determinedly, began to edge herself upward. I helped her where I could, grabbing a leg, a hip, an armpit. Finally she was up there on the tiled roof with me.

I let my eyes go over the roof, that tilted sharply, then ran down in a slope toward the rooftop of the adjoining house. From there the way seemed easy enough, the roofs there were flat.

"Just give me a few seconds to catch my breath," she whispered.

I was glad enough of the chance to get my own breathing apparatus back into shape. The gunshots had ceased, I heard the roar of motors, the screech of tires as somebody peeled off.

Donna said, "They've stopped fighting and run. Bocca and the others will find the don. They'll look for us."

"That they will, honey. I'm supposed to be locked up safe in a room back there. Bocca will find the open window. He'll know where we are."

She stirred. "We'd better get going, then."

I scrambled on hands and knees along that sloping roof, slipping at times but making it to the ridge. Here I crawled on along even more carefully, if possible. One slip and I'd go tumbling down that tiled slope like Jill down the hill to wind up with a broken body in the alleyway. I made it, finally, to the edge of the far side where I could see a row of flat rooftops waiting for me.

I turned my head.

Donna was halfway along that roof, moving slowly, inch by inch. She was scared silly, I could see it in her big eyes and white face. But she was gritty, she wasn't quitting. She didn't dare quit, if she wanted to stay alive. I turned, offered her my hand, after a time. She shook her head, tried to smile.

I half slid, half ran down the last slope and made it to the edge. It was a jump of maybe three feet to the flat roof across the narrow alley. I made it, so did Donna. After that, it was easy, all we had to do was run.

When we came to the last roof, we looked at each other. The same thought was in both our minds. We had to get on the ground, alive and in one piece. And, as if to add to our woes, we could hear Francesco Galuppo and Petey boy bellowing down in the street.

"Donna! Donna! Where are you?"

"Donna answer us!"

Her hand caught my forearm. She was actually shaking. "They'll kill us," she whimpered. All I could do was pat her hand consolingly. I felt the same way she did. As soon as they caught sight of us, they'd begin shooting.

They would have found their don dead, by now, they must have guessed that either Donna or I had done it, there wasn't anybody else. When they saw us together, they'd know damn well we were in cahoots.

We tiptoed to the edge of the roof, peered down.

I saw a row of tin roofs, the tops of storage sheds, that made fine stepping stones, if we could reach them. The nearest was about twelve feet down. It had one advantage: it was a flat roof.

I slipped off my slacks, showing my bare legs and black nylon panties that just about managed to hide my private parts. Donna eyed me hungrily, her stare avid.

"You hold one end of these, Donna," I told her, inching forward to the edge of the roof. "And for Pete's sake, don't let go. I'm going to grab hold of the other end and lower myself as far as I can go. I'll have to drop the rest of the way, but this will be a help."

"What about me?" she breathed.

"I'll be down there to break your fall, to help you a little, so it won't be such a drop. Now come on. It's our only hope."

She nodded, biting her lower lip, caught the belt part of the slacks and fastened both hands on it. I went over the edge, playing out the slacks, then I let go.

For a minute, I thought Donna was going to come pitching over the eave on top of me, but she drove her heels at the leader and it held. I hung at the end of those slacks for a few seconds, then let go. The drop wasn't so bad. I landed and tumbled, caught myself, and got to my feet.

Donna's frightened face peered down at me. "You all right?"

"No bones broken. Now come on! Throw down the slacks, then drop toward me."

She was scared, and I didn't blame her. She threw the slacks, I caught them in midair, then watched as first one stockinged leg came over the leader, showing me a delightful length of hosiery and bare thighmeat, and then the other. For a second, as Donna poised with her legs apart, I could see right up between them. She wore no panties, just a garterbelt, and her hairy nooky nest was something to make a guy or a gal drool.

I shook myself back to the moment. No time now for dwelling on genital goodies. My hands went up as far as I could reach. I said, "Drop down, Donna— but try to lean against the wall. I'm going to catch your feet in my hands, if I can."

She let go, she came down hard with her feet toward my palms. She didn't look like a heavy girl, but there was plenty of meat on her frame; when it landed on my upheld hands, my knees buckled and I came close to collapsing. But my legs held up, and Donna leaned against the wall with her arms, peering down at me.

"You all right?" she called.

This was no time to carry on a conversation, so I kept my mouth shut. I started to bend my knees, lowering her. After a moment she told me she could jump. She did, and I caught her, holding her upright.

We both leaned against the wall, getting our breath.

If Petey or Bocca or any of the others had come around the corner of this building, we'd have been dead ducks. I finally pushed away from the building wall and slid legs into my slacks. I made sure the Luger was in the belt, then moved to the edge of this flat roof.

A sloping tin roof was about five feet below this one. There was a smaller roof below that, then came the blessed ground. "We can make it from here easily enough. Let's go."

It was a matter of inching our fannies to the edge of the tin plate, then dropping. In a few seconds, we were on the ground.

Donna asked, "Where do we go from here?"

"We steal a car, if we can find one."

Donna frowned thoughtfully, muttered, "Bocca has a car, a beautiful Fiat. It's his pride and joy. He keeps it somewhere down here, but we'll need a key."

"I can start a motor without a key, by crossing wires," I grinned. "You know where it is, you lead the way."

I followed her quivering behind in the black maid's uniform she was wearing, along the row of building walls. She had torn the skirt of one of the rooftops, she'd taken out a section of the black stuff, so that she showed her legs all the way up to her bare thighs as she moved.

We came to a building that had been converted into a garage. Donna waved me to silence, put her hand on the knob and opened the door. She slipped inside.

Then I heard Bocca's voice. "Where the hell've you been?"

"I—I was a-afraid. I ran out of the house."

"Little fool! Have you seen Cherry?"

I moved my feet so I got inside the garage, too. Bocca heard me, he whirled, his Walthian Beretta came up. But the Luger was in my hand and I fired first. I saw a hole come into his chest, right about where his heart was, a small hole, very neat until the blood started oozing from it.

He was dead on his feet, staring at me. The Beretta was halfway up, it quivered in his hand. Then it sank slowly downward to his side. Almost in the same motion, he twisted sideways and his body fell at Donna's feet.

She started at him disbelievingly.

The noise of the Luger had been deafening. I yelled, "Don't just stand there, get into his car." My feet took me to the wall where I pressed a button. The door swung up on silent hinges.

Then I was sliding my rump onto the driver's seat and reaching for the ignition key in the lock. The motor throbbed to powerful life. Donna squawked and ran for the Fiat. As she came in, my eyes touched the fuel gauge. It was full to the very top.

We went out of the garage in a shower of flying pebbles. I headed the two-seater convertible down the alley which was just wide enough for it. I tipped over a couple of refuse cans, but who can be neat at such a time? When I came to the alley's end, I was doing forty miles an hour.

I swept out onto the Rue Bravade, and stepped down hard on the gas pedal. These Fiats can do ninety miles an hour when they have to, and I was happy to discover that Bocca Carducci had kept his car tuned and ready, as if for a Grand Prix race.

Donna sat beside me, legs crossed and showing plenty of stocking and bared thighs, but she had a big grin on her face. After a time, she turned toward me.

"You are a very good shot, Cherry. That Luger bullet took him right in the heart." There was a question in her voice.

"Joe Turessi liked me to be able to take care of myself, honey. He insisted I learn how to use a rod. I used to practice a lot."

She was staring at me thoughtfully, I saw with a sideways glance. It was almost as if she didn't know quite what to make of me. After a time she said, "Italian girls are not trained this way. The men think we're useless except in a bed."

"Male chauvinist pigs," I nodded.

She hadn't the slightest idea of what I was talking about, but this made no difference, because she was like my eyes, she kept turning this way and that, nodding from time to time.

"I think we have shaken them off," she murmured at last.

"We got away clean, if that's what you mean."

"Not clean, no. I saw a man with binoculars watching us when we came out of the alleyway."

"You sure of that?"

"I'm sure. He will be the Countess' man, right? The same one who watched you at the party, probably."

"And he'll get word to the Countess. Donna, where does this road go? Do you know?"

"Toward Cannes, I believe. Though it joins the coast road a little further on."

I guided the Fiat along a narrow winding road between fields of thyme and lavender, past low stone fences that bordered meadows where cows grazed, and a few sheep. It was a peaceful scene, it was hard to believe that Donna and I were fleeing for our lives with an invention that might threaten the power structure of the whole damn world.

The smell of the *garrique*—that special blend of scents that comes from the juniper resin, thyme and lavender, was all around us. In the distance we could make out the red earth of this corner of Provence, neatly divided into the quadrangles where vegetables are grown, and a melon patch here and there. We swept on, we had no time to spare for sightseeing. But the countryside was all around us, it seemed ridiculous that somewhere behind us a car or maybe two or three, was filled with killers lusting for our blood.

Where Donna told me, I avoided the coast road, turning left onto a spur that took us up into more or less mountainous country, the beginnings of the Maritime Alps. Ahead was a stretch of rocky ground farming land where vegetables grew, dotted here and there with woven split bamboo screens called cannisses that protect the fields against the mistral. This mistral dominates the thinking of the Provencal farmer. It is a cold, northerly wind strong enough to overturn trains, and will sweep the rich loam from the earth unless the ground is protected.

Donna whispered, "They are coming. I see them now."

"Can you make out who it is?"

"Francesco Galuppo—with Petey."

I thought about the Luger I'd taken from the don. I'd fired it once. If its clips had been full when it first came into my hands, it still held seven bullets. Enough to handle Frankie and Petey, I figured.

"The hell with this cops and robbers stuff," I told Donna. "We're going to make a stand." My hands swung the wheel, the Fiat lurched to the left, onto a rocky slope, and began to climb.

"What are you going to do?" she gasped, hanging on as the car bumped and skidded upward.

"Shoot to kill," I said grimly.

I shut off the motor, hopped out, yelling to the girl to follow me, and headed my feet toward a little highland bound about with boulders. Those rocks would be like stone walls behind which to hide. When I reached the top, I saw that there was a flat bit of ground between the boulders.

I ran for it, waited as Donna came up between two big stones, then said, "Nobody can get at us here. We can sweep the whole countryside from this place."

A wink of sunlight on metal showed me where the Mercedes-Benz was coming fast. If Frankie and Petey were in that car, where was Tony, the other muscleman? Bocca was dead, I didn't have to worry about him. Probably Tony was dead, too, or he'd have been there with Francesco Galuppo.

Frankie saw the Fiat stopped on the side of the

hill and veered in to the side of the road. I settled my frame on a flat piece of rock and lifted the Luger into my right hand. The two men came out of the car, peered up at our rock fortress and ran for cover. I saw Frankie plop down behind a fallen tree.

"Cherry!" he yelled. "Let's make a deal. The Countess is right behind us—she's following me the way I followed you. And she's got six men with her. Maybe even seven."

Six men! My heart sank. With Francesco Galuppo and Petey, that made eight enemies I had to kill. I only had seven bullets.

Chapter Eight

Even if I made every shot a kill, there wouldn't be enough cartridges to do the job. That was when I started sweating. But I choked back my fears, I had to play the string out all the way.

"No deals," I yelled.

A bullet chipped the rock beside my head, singing shrilly as it went off into the air. I turned my eyes to the north. Petey had made a flanking movement, he was below me in a stand of wild olive trees. I squirmed around, flat on the ground, and put my left hand to my right, to support the Luger. I was hidden from Frankie by the rocks. I waited with the patience of a cat.

There was movement below. I saw the sleeve of a shirt, a bare arm. There was no more sound.

Donna whispered, "Cherry! Cherry! Francesco is running up the hill."

No time to think about him. If I pivoted for him, Petey would get even closer. He had to move. When he saw Frankie running without opposition, Petey would feel he was safe. He had to! Come on, come on, damn you! Make your move so I can finish you off, at least.

My heart thudded. I did not breathe.

Ahhhh! Petey stepped out from behind the gnarled bole of the olive tree. His face had a big grin on it. He came charging right at the slope and the boulders behind which we were hidden. The Luger moved, I trailed him with his big chest framed in my sight. My finger squeezed the trigger. The Luger jumped.

Petey stopped as if a hand had shoved him back. He stared down at his chest where the lead had caught him. He started to go backwards slowly. He fell and lay there. Behind me, Donna whimpered.

I swung around.

She had been watching what happened to Petey, I think this was only the second time in her life she'd seen a man killed. Her face was very white.

I paid her no never mind. I squidgled my way around on the rocks until I was looking down the slope. There was no sign of Francesco Galuppo. I got nervous. I made it to my feet, ran to another rock. No sign of him. Where in hell was that guy?

I heard the sound of car motors.

Then a shadow darkened the rock where I leaned.

I whirled. Frankie was coming through an opening between two boulders, his eyes taking in the scene almost instantly. His Walthian Beretta swung in my direction.

He fired. A bullet touched the rock beside my arm.

Frankie had fired wildly. He hadn't known where I was when he'd come through that opening, he'd had to get off his shot before I could fire at him. But he was moving fast, he couldn't halt himself to plant his body for a better shot.

My feet were on firm ground. My target was in front of me, looming as big as one of the boulders. The Luger came up. I didn't even have to aim. All I needed to do was pull the trigger.

Donna screamed.

Frankie went backward off his feet, slamming into one of the rocks behind him. His side hit the stone, his arm that held the Beretta came up high as if he were trying to wave. But at the moment of impact—even as I jumped forward to grab it—his automatic went sailing into the air and over the boulder.

"Get his gun, Donna," I panted.

The girl couldn't move. Her eyes were huge where she stared at the Mafia *capo* as he slid down the rock, dead. His body crumpled and fell to its base.

I dove through the opening myself. I could see the Walthian Beretta about a dozen feet away, waiting for my eager little paw to pick it up.

I also saw two cars braking to a stop on the road below. The Countess came out of one, three men got out of the car she'd been driving. From the other car stepped four more.

She saw me crouched frozen in front of the boulders. Whether she suspected what I was after, I didn't know. But she lifted her arm and pointed. The men with her had their guns in their hands. They lifted them and blazed away at me.

Why they didn't hit me, I'll never know. Bullets dug divots from the ground and hit stones all around me. One even went past my car. I'd never make it to that gun on the ground ahead of me, my mind told me, so I dove back between the rocks.

My eyes touched the body of Francesco Galuppo. Donna was on her hands and knees beside him, her fingers running through his pockets. "Bullets, maybe he had more bullets on him," she whispered to me.

I smiled faintly at her. "Good thinking, honey, but those bullets won't fit the Luger."

She shook her head. "There aren't any, anyhow."

Making my run to the smallest opening between the boulders, I flopped bellydown and raised my head. The six men were walking up the slope, the Countess following at a more leisurely pace. I could hardly believe my eyes. Apparently, since I'd made my run for Frankie's gun, they thought all I had to defend myself was an empty gun.

I raised the Luger, put both hands on its butt. I sighted on the nearest man, fired. I turned the Luger barrel to the next, held steady for a second and again squeezed the trigger.

The two men I'd fired at dropped like stones. The others yelled and began running down the slope, waving their arms like crazy. The Countess didn't wait to ask questions. She turned and ran as fast as her shapely gams would take her.

"Now!" I yelled at Donna. "Get the Beretta! I'll cover them, their backs are turned, they won't even see you."

She ran like an Olympic sprinter, bent over and churning her legs. I could not see her, I was too busy watching the Countess and her boys, doing some mental calculations in my head. Five men yet to kill and me with only four bullets left.

One of the men turned, saw Donna, brought his gun up. At the same time I heard Donna scream.

I ran to the opening between the boulders, saw her flat on the ground. My eyes touched the men and the Countess. Leaving the security of the rocks meant I was offering my bod to their marksmanship, but I couldn't leave Donna out there, not without learning if she were alive or dead.

So I ducked low and beat feet in her direction. The men were turning now, lifting their revolvers and automatics. I made a beautiful target. They fired. The bullets sang around my head and shoulders as I threw myself flat within touching distance of the girl. My hand shook her. She stirred, opened her eyelids.

Terror dawned inside her brown eyes.

"You hurt bad?" I asked.

"Hurt? No, I—I don't think so." She flushed. "I—I think I fainted."

A bullet hit dirt between us. I pivoted, lifted the Luger, steadied it, squeezed off a shot. The four men with the Countess were losing their fear, they'd turned with us on the ground before them. My bullet caught a man in his throat. Redness erupted with a gout of blood as he twisted and dropped.

That made the others more cautious, they turned and ran for cover, despite the curses the Countess threw at them. My hand shook Donna. "Now! On your feet while their backs are turned. Come on! And—don't forget the Beretta!"

We made it between the rocks, Donna with the Italian automatic in her grip. We threw ourselves face down on the ground and lay there, damn grateful to be alive.

I saw shadows all around me when I lifted my head. The sun was setting beyond Languedoc to the west, and my heart sank with it. In the dark, when we couldn't see them, the boys with the Countess would come crawling up the hill. I think Donna realized it at the same time, because she looked at me with her worry clear to see.

"I know, honey," I told her. "It'll be night in a while and then they'll come for us."

"What can we do?"

"Wait for it. What else?"

But I had a plan in mind. If I couldn't see them when they were crawling up the slope they couldn't see me crawling down it. And I'd be all kinds of a horse's ass if I stayed here for them to come and shoot me. So I went to an opening between the boulders and propped myself there, seeing that the *comtesse* and her little army had taken cover.

Night was forever in getting to us, but when it formed a blackness with only the stars overhead to furnish any light, I tapped Donna. "Let's get going. We're not staying here for them to crawl up and shoot us. Can you move quietly?"

I barely saw her nod. Then I was sliding snakelike between the rocks and onto the slope. I had tucked the Luger into my slacks belt, I had my lipstick in my hand. I went along the ground very slowly, keeping my head as low as I could, hoping to see a body framed against the night sky.

We were halfway down the hill when I heard pebbles grate. I froze and lifted the lethal lipstick. A man was less than five feet away, moving slowly. I raised the lipstick, aimed it and twisted the base.

The man grunted, then was quiet. I think he believed a rock had pinched him, because in a moment, he started crawling again, but slowly. He did not crawl far, he just put his head on the ground and died.

Donna didn't know what had happened, she was some distance behind me. I crawled down a little further.

Then Donna screamed. She must have come face to face with the dead man and didn't know he was dead.

That was all the signal the Countess' boys needed. Their guns started blasting, cutting red streaks in the night. I rolled over and over down the slope, as their guns—there were only the three of them, now—sprayed lead where I'd just been.

I slowed my roll, began crawling up the slope. I was behind them, they weren't expecting an attack from this direction. As long as I kept quiet, I'd be safe enough. I saw a man in front of me, head raised and peering to his left. The lipstick came up. I fired.

The man jerked. He looked around him in surprise, but I was flat to the ground again, now. He reached behind him to where the pellet had gone into him. Then he gave a yell and got to his feet, and began running. I heard voices call to him. I spotted those voices, I abandoned the lipstick for the Luger.

The other two men were lifting their heads, staring at their companions as if he'd gone mad, the way he was running and screaming. I think he felt the death inside him, moving along his veins. But I had no eyes for him. I studied those heads in the sights of my automatic and squeezed the trigger. Fast. Too fast. I missed. I had two shots left. I had to make them count. I steadied my hands. They died with my bullets going through their skulls.

After this, there was a long silence. The Countess was somewhere below, I felt sure, maybe at the cars. She couldn't know what had happened, though she'd heard Donna scream and seen the red gun flashes in the dark night. Maybe she was up on the slope, but from the way she'd stayed behind when her boys attacked, I figured she was down there, where it was reasonably safe.

I crawled down the slope on hands and knees. She was standing in front of one of the cars, a Porsche, straining her eyes to see what was going on. The awful silence after the exchange of gunfire was probably shredding her nerves. I would dearly have loved to talk to her, to get answers to some questions about her, but it was more important that I get that instant hypnotic device back to Uncle Sam country. I inched forward as her dark body got bigger and bigger, and my hand raised the lipstick. The empty Luger was in my belt.

I didn't know the range of the airgun I held, so I crawled even closer. Maybe she saw me then, because her head lowered and her eyes seemed to gleam almost ferally, like a cat's. I twisted the lipstick base, there was the soft plop of released air and the Countess doubled up, both hands going to her belly.

I hopped up and ran to her, afraid she might have a gun on her somewhere and use it. She moaned, holding herself, too concerned with the fact that she was hurt to bother about trying to kill me. My hands went over her, she made no resistance. She was clean.

I caught her when she started to sag, saying, "I'm sorry, it was you or me."

"The don?" she whispered. "Benito Castraccia?"

"Dead. The same way you're dying."

To my surprise she smiled happily, nodding her head. "Good, good. That bastard—he killed my—son. Caught him holding back a payment, had him—weighted down with stones and thrown alive into the sea."

She was dying, her body was getting heavier and heavier. I lowered her to the ground, trying to make her last moments as comfortable as possible. She opened her eyes after a while, looked up at me.

"You're some—girl, Cherry. I wished I'd had you with—me. As it is—I'll be seeing you sooner—sooner than you think."

Saying which, she gave a convulsive shudder and died.

I got to my feet. I didn't know whether Donna was still alive or not, so I had to find her. But she came staggering down the slope just then, weaving a little as if drunk. The Walthian Beretta was still in her hand.

She came to stand beside the Countess, staring down at her. "She was an ambitious woman," she said softly. "She thought she was going to take over the Family."

"You knew her?"

Donna smiled. "I heard rumors. The don killed her son, and that set her off. She had money, she used it to buy herself a mob of her own. This is the result."

She looked at me inquiringly. "What now?"

"We go find a bed to sleep in. Not back in Saint Tropez, some little inn or farmhouse, whatever we can find."

She nodded, walked with me toward the Fiat. I wanted out of here fast, I didn't want any French gendarmes finding dead bodies with me in the vicinity and still alive. We slid into the Fiat and split.

It was close to dawn when we eased to a stop in front of a little country inn, with a wooden sign hanging in front of it and a pale light burning before its door. We banged on that door for about ten minutes before it opened and a Frenchwoman, holding her bathrobe about her, stared at us coldly.

"A bedroom," I begged. "We've been driving all night, and we're exhausted."

She spat some French cusswords at us, and made to slam the door in our faces. I had the answer for that. I waved a hundred new franc notes in her beady little eyes. She got the greedy gleam I'd figured on, since the normal charge for a bedroom was maybe two bucks American and since the hundred franc note represented a little more than twenty. Her hand grabbed. I went through the door with Donna before she could change her mind. She asked about luggage but I said we just wanted to sleep.

Her shoulders shrugged as she led us upstairs and into a bedroom.

No sooner had the door shut behind her than I peeled off my tan pullover sweater and shucked out of my slacks. I tossed my empty Luger onto the bureau and left my lipstick beside it. Then with only my black nylon panties and the wired bra on, I dove for the bed, yanking down the covers and slipping my bare legs under them. I pulled the covers up and was about to close my eyes when I saw Donna standing there with her ruined maid's uniform on, looking at me in puzzlement.

"What's the matter?" I asked. "You're not worried, are you? The whole affair is finished and done with. Tomorrow sometime, after a good sleep for a day and a night and a steak dinner, we'll fly back to the United States. All your troubles are over, Donna."

She nodded and started running down her uniform zipper. I turned over and lay on my side, ready for sleep. That was the last thing I knew for a long time.

When I woke, it was to the touch of gentle fingers on my naked breasts. My eyelids quivered, opened. I was lying on my back, my breasts were bare and hard, the nipples were standing up, and Donna was using her soft wet mouth on them, moving from one big nipple to the other, licking them with her tongue, kissing them tenderly, then taking each swollen brown nubbin between her lips to suck.

My hips moved in heat. There was a wetness between my thighs that showed the Italian girl was getting to me. Her mouth was very hot, very hungry as she nursed at my breasts, slowly and with moaning delight.

Dawn was in the air, I saw as my blurry stare touched the windows. We must have slept for a day and a night. No wonder Donna was filled with so much erotic energy! I let a smile touch my mouth, my hands move to her head. My fingers rubbed her scalp as they held her long brown hair.

"Darling," I whispered. "What a way to wake up."

"I saw you lying here beside me, saw how beautiful you are. I had to unhook your brassiere, take these out to play with them."

"Go on, don't stop."

She lay half over me. I could feel her naked body, softly fleshed and bed-warmed, close against my own. My hand ran down her spine to her buttocks. I let my fingernails move over each swelling mound, down the anal crease. When I reached the furry little nest of her genitals, I toyed gently with the slick flesh nestling between her hairs.

"Oh! Oh, my God," she whimpered, hips jerking, legs sliding apart. "It's been so long, so long for me, Cherry. You have no idea. And, Cherry—*sono pazzo per te!* I'm crazy about you!"

Her lips left my rock-hard breasts, slipped down my belly. A tonguetip tickled my navel, then slid lower even as she hooked her fingers in my black nylon panties. I lifted a leg, then the other. I was naked and exposed to her. For a long moment she remained like that, staring at my scarlet pansy hidden in those red curls. Then she gave a little sigh and leaned forward, her mouth open. She came right down on it and I had to fight from yelling with excitement. A tongue came out and ran about my labia, found my stiff clitoral bud and worked on it. I was in heaven. I damn near died from delight. My hips were moving up and down and around, my hands were in her thick brown hair to keep her at her devotions. My breasts shook like white jelly to my movements and my head moved back and forth on the pillow with lazy slowness. She was making me forget everything, all the gunplay and the killing, the agony I'd endured. She was making it all worthwhile.

After I'd spent myself half a dozen times, I realized she must be in exquisite agony, herself. She would want the delights of a loving tongue, the caresses of my fingers.

"Up here, Donna," I whispered. "Turn around."

Her head came up, lips wet with my excitement, her eyes wild with the *faire minette* fever. She stood, stepped forward, stood above my face with her legs spread apart. Donna was wet betwen her thighs, there was that same wetness on her inner thighs. Slowly she bent her knees, lowering herself.

She was perfumed, scented. I was a little surprised. Had she had time to take a bath or a shower? What had she been doing since she'd crawled into bed with me last night? It seemed a little strange. . .

Then I gave over thinking as her wide wet lips came down around my mouth and tongue. My hands slid up her sides, touched her breasts, stroked and fondled them. In seconds she was jerking, mewling, panting.

How long we lay like that, I'm not sure. After a time, Donna crawled off and gave a little sigh. "It's been wonderful, Cherry—just marvelous. It's too bad it has to end."

"No need for that, you're coming to America, we can see each other now and then."

"I'm—afraid not."

I had been lying there with my eyes closed, just basking. Something about her tone of voice made me open my eyes fast. Donna was standing alongside the bed with the Walthian Beretta in her hand. The gun was aimed at little old me.

"Donna! What is this?"

I sat up and she backed off. "Just move slowly, Cherry. Real slowly. You see, I want that gadget, the instant hypnotizer. I'm going to sell it to the highest bidder."

I stared at her, thoughts whirling. How did she know what it was, unless—? Sure, sure. It all added up. "You're the spy," I said slowly. "That's how the Countess learned about the gadget. You told her. She put you in the house with Bocca and Frankie boy, as a maid. You heard everything that was going on, you told *la comtesse* about it, and—and you were going into the room after the don when he was hiding the thing to kill him and to steal it."

She gave me a tight smile. "You're smart, Cherry."

"Only you saw he was dead and you figured I'd taken it, right?"

"You did take it. You had to. It wasn't in the box or in the safe."

I relaxed, lying flat on the bed. "If I did, I'm certainly not carrying it around with me now." My hand waved idly. "I'm lying here stark naked. And it isn't in my pussy, either. As you know."

She smiled faintly, having explored that pussy with fingers and tongue. "No, it isn't there. So where is it?"

"Back in the house, in the room where I killed the don."

She snapped a curse word. *"Macche!* Do you think

I'm a fool?"

I slid a bare leg toward her. "May I get out of bed? I'd like to put something on." I brought my nylon panties with me, waved them at her. As she nodded, I slid my legs into the holes, stood and pulled them up, wriggling my hips and letting my breasts dance. She eyed them appreciatively, but something about her told me she wasn't going to get distracted. I left the wired bra on the bed, moved toward the bureau.

"The Luger is empty," she mocked me.

My hand lifted the lipstick instead. I remembered she'd never actually seen me use it, held it up so she could see it. "No, I just wanted to do my lips. If I have to die here, I want to look good for the mortician."

Even while I was talking, I turned the base of the special weapon. The air popped and Donna blinked. I'd made a clean hit in the soft flesh of her belly. Before she could recover from her surprise, I dove. That instant of pain distracted her long enough for the edge of my hand to sweep in against her gun wrist. The Walthian Beretta went flying.

At almost the same moment, I hit her with the edge of my other hand against her soft throat. Her eyes rolled back in her head and she crumpled up on the floor. In a few seconds, she would be dead.

I dove for the bed, grabbed the wired bra.

In that room on the Rue Bravade with the dead don, when I'd been trying to think of a fitting hiding place for that thin steel rod with the lens, I'd decided on the brassiere. I'd slipped out one of the wires, replaced it with the hypnotizer. Sure, sure, it hurt a little bit when I tried to do some acrobatics and such, but it was worth an occasional pinch or two to make sure it was safe.

Not even Donna had suspected it. She'd undone my bra this morning without the slightest suspicion of the treasure inside it. Had she known, I'd be the dead one right now, instead of her. I checked the bra. The thing was still there. I lifted the C cups, slid my breasts into them, then reached behind me to hook it up.

On came my tan pullover sweater and beige slacks. I left the Luger where it was, but I did pick up the Walthian Beretta and slid it into a slacks pocket along with my lethal lipstick.

The concierge or landlady or whatever her name was, was downstairs, waiting as I appeared. I smiled at her, lifted out my wallet and forced five of the new twenty franc notes on her. A hundred bucks American.

"The other one will sleep for a while. I'm going to go meet a friend. I'll be back by nightfall."

I don't know whether she believed me, I really didn't care. I would be at the Nice airport in a few hours, and all the concierge had to go on was the license number of the Fiat, which was in the name of Bocca Carducci.

She squinted at me oddly, but she nodded even as her hands went around the new francs. I walked out into the Riviera sunshine and headed for the car. I drove away, telling myself not to eat until I was on board a big TWA jetliner taking me stateside. It was worth the lack of food for a few more hours to be able to say in Italian, *"Ho vinto!"*

I had won!

TO THE READER

If you enjoyed this book, you will be glad to know that there are many others just as well written, just as interesting, to be had in the Fiction House Press Library.

You will find the Fiction House Press Library online at

www.FictionHousePress.com

www.ingramcontent.com/pod-product-compliance
Lightning Source LLC
Chambersburg PA
CBHW060400030726
47497CB00003B/794